"It doesn't bother me that you've thought about sleeping with me."

She'd only gotten the words out by studying the decorative marble backsplash behind the six-burner stove. This let her detach from the intensity of the exchange. "With our proximity..." She shrugged. "It only makes sense that you'd consider it."

Linc was silent for what felt like minutes, but based on the rapid thump of her heart was more like seconds.

"I think you're discounting how important you are to me. You and Honey." His fingertips grazed her knuckles. The fleeting touch awakened a flock of butterflies in her stomach. "Have I thought about you in that way? Sure. But you know I'd never take advantage of our situation in that way."

"What if you weren't taking advantage?"

"Claire." He sounded half amused and half despairing.

"Do you want to?"

"Claire." This time when he said her name there was a warning in it. His fingers gripped her bare shoulders, sending shock waves of longing searing through her. "You have no idea what you do to me."

* * *

Upstairs Downstairs Baby is part of Harlequin Desire's #1 bestselling series, Billionaires and Babies: Powerful men...wrapped around their babies' little fingers.

Dear Reader,

Whenever I start a new series it's always exciting, but never more so than when I get to set the stories in a place where I long to visit. One of the best things about reading is being transported to a place either real or imagined. The same can be said for writing. Inspired by the reality show *Southern Charm*, I wanted to submerge myself in the gorgeous city of Charleston, South Carolina.

Behind the doors of the gorgeous historic homes south of Broad, ten generations of proper Charleston men and women have weathered economic downturns while clinging to their tight society. If you're an outsider, good luck breaking into the inner circles. This is what housekeeper Claire Robbins understands long before she falls in love with her handsome, professional baseball player boss, Linc Thurston.

I had so much fun watching them fall in love from opposite sides of the social line carved deep into the bedrock of the city. I hope you enjoy their story.

All the best,

Cat Schield

CAT SCHIELD

———

UPSTAIRS DOWNSTAIRS BABY

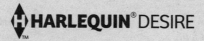
HARLEQUIN® DESIRE

Recycling programs
for this product may
not exist in your area.

ISBN-13: 978-1-335-97143-2

Upstairs Downstairs Baby

Printed in U.S.A.

Cat Schield has been reading and writing romance since high school. Although she graduated from college with a BA in business, her idea of a perfect career was writing books for Harlequin. And now, after winning the Romance Writers of America 2010 Golden Heart® Award for Best Contemporary Series Romance, that dream has come true. Cat lives in Minnesota with her daughter, Emily, and their Burmese cat. When she's not writing sexy, romantic stories for Harlequin Desire, she can be found sailing with friends on the St. Croix River, or in more exotic locales, like the Caribbean and Europe. She loves to hear from readers. Find her at catschield.net and follow her on Twitter, @catschield.

Books by Cat Schield

Harlequin Desire

Upstairs Downstairs Baby

The Sherdana Royals

Royal Heirs Required
A Royal Baby Surprise
Secret Child, Royal Scandal

Las Vegas Nights

At Odds with the Heiress
A Merger by Marriage
A Taste of Temptation
The Black Sheep's Secret Child
Little Secret, Red Hot Scandal
The Heir Affair

Visit her Author Profile page at Harlequin.com, or catschield.net, for more titles!

Prologue

Everly Briggs made sure she gave every appearance of listening sympathetically as London McCaffrey imparted her romantic woes. They were attending the "Beautiful Women Taking Charge" networking event, featuring a keynote from Poppy Hart, a motivational speaker and owner of Hart Success Counseling.

"And he gave you no reason for breaking off your engagement?" Everly sounded aghast, though in truth, she already knew all about London's failed romance with professional baseball player Linc Thurston. It was the reason she'd contrived to meet her tonight.

London pressed her coral-tinted lips into a thin line as she shook her head. "He claims he isn't ready to get married, but we've been engaged for two years."

Everly tried not to wince at London's affected Southern accent. The beautiful woman, with her silky straight blond hair and expensive clothes, was originally from Connecticut and that made her an outsider here in Charleston.

"Do you think he was cheating on you?" Zoe Crosby asked, her light brown eyes blazing with outrage from inside their frame of dark, lush lashes.

"Linc…cheat?" London toyed with her string of Mikimoto pearls as she considered this. "Yes, I suppose that's a possibility. He travels more than half the year with the team and lives in Texas during the season."

"And you know how women love professional sports players," Zoe added. "My former brother-in-law is a race car driver and has women after him all the time."

"These men have no right to treat us so badly," Everly said. Each of the three women had shared a tale of being wronged by a wealthy, powerful man. "We need to get back at all of them. Linc, Tristan and Ryan. They all need to be taught a lesson."

"As much as the idea appeals to me," London said, "I can't imagine taking revenge on Linc without it blowing up in my face."

"What good would it do any of us? Anything we try would only end up making us look bad," Zoe said, echoing London.

"Not if we go after each other's men." Everly restrained a smug smile as she took in her companions' curious expressions. "Think about it. We're strangers at a cocktail party. Who would ever connect us? I go after Linc. London goes after Tristan. And, Zoe, you go after Ryan."

"When you say 'go after,'" Zoe said, sounding hesitant even as her head bobbed eagerly, "what do you have in mind?"

"We're not going to do them bodily harm," Everly said with a silvery laugh. "But there's no reason why we couldn't ruin a business deal or mess with their current relationship. We've each been the victim of a ruthless man. And yet we're strong, empowered women. Don't you think it's time we acted like it?"

London started nodding right along with Zoe. "I like the idea of striking back at Linc. He deserves to feel a little of the pain and humiliation I've endured since our engagement ended."

Zoe leaned forward. "Count me in, too."

"Marvelous. Now, here's what I think we should do…"

One

He needed to fire Claire.

Lincoln Thurston opened his mouth to do just that as she set his morning smoothie of kale, protein powder and blueberries on the breakfast bar near his gym bag. Then she gave him a smile of such sweetness that he was helpless to do anything but grin back.

Letting his housekeeper go was a matter of desperation. He was obsessed with the lovely young woman who cooked and cleaned for him. Over the twelve months since he'd hired her, it had become increasingly difficult to avoid thinking about her in a certain way. A certain carnal way. Which was why he absolutely, positively couldn't have her living in his house another day.

And yet he felt responsible for her welfare the way he did for his mother and sister. Claire was almost three thousand miles from her family and her husband had been killed in Afghanistan two years earlier. Besides, what excuse could he give? She cooked like a dream and kept his Charleston house in perfect order. And she was more than his housekeeper. She cared about him. Him. Linc Thurston, the regular guy. Not Linc Thurston, the ballplayer or the multimillionaire or the recently single and highly eligible bachelor.

Linc gave his head a brisk shake. He had to stop thinking about Claire as if she meant something to him. It had already proved detrimental to his love life, causing him to end his engagement.

Not that it was fair to blame Claire. She was the perfect employee. She never once encouraged him or acted as if she was even aware that he was an attractive, financially stable man who could take her away from the drudgery of her current occupation. It was refreshing that she wasn't working an angle, and yet part of him wished that seduction was her goal. He wouldn't have minded being at the heart of her sinister plot to trap him. At least then he could sleep with her and never for a second regret it.

As a shortstop with the Texas Barons, making fifteen million a year, Linc was accustomed to having women throw themselves at him. Not even his engagement had slowed them down. At twenty-six, when he was at the beginning of his eight-year, nine-figure contract, he'd basked in the attention. Now, at thirty-three, with only one year left to go, he wanted to settle down with a wife and kids. Or that had been the plan, until he'd reevaluated his feelings for London McCaffrey and realized he wasn't in love with her.

So, what was it about Claire that preoccupied him?

"Mama."

The reason Linc would be the biggest jerk of all time if he fired Claire ran into the kitchen buck naked.

"Where are your clothes?" Claire exclaimed as her daughter streaked past.

With her straight shoulder-length brown hair and a sprinkling of freckles over her nose, Claire had a fresh girl-next-door look that sometimes made her seem too young to be the mother of a toddler.

Two-year-old Honey Robbins made a beeline for Linc. He scooped her into his arms, whirling her around. She was a bright-eyed, enthusiastic charmer who'd wrapped him around her finger from their first meeting. Honey shrieked with laughter, and he smiled. Mother and daughter had burrowed beneath his skin to such an extent that not having them around would be so much worse than his constant battle with attraction.

He would just have to endure.

"I don't know what it is about this child that she can't manage to keep her clothes on," Claire said, her brown eyes fixed on the toddler's chubby cheeks.

"Maybe she takes after her mother?" Had he just said that? His careless words put bright spots of color in Claire's cheeks and inappropriate thoughts in his head. "I don't mean that you can't keep your clothes on," he hastened to add. "It's just something people say. I mean, about children taking after their parents."

"Well, that's a relief," Claire said. "I thought maybe

the security cameras caught me skinny-dipping last week."

In truth, there were no security cameras and there was no way Claire would take her clothes off and slip naked into his pool. Which was why she could joke about it. Despite the provocative nature of the banter, Claire was a very proper and modest twenty-seven-year-old widow who still wore her wedding band. She obviously wasn't over her husband, a hero who'd died two years earlier when a suicide bomber attacked his military convoy.

"I guess I better go review the video," he said, filling his voice with lighthearted good humor. "What day might that have been?"

"I'm not gonna tell you." Her grin wasn't flirtatious, merely one of standard amusement. "It'll give you something to do while I'm vacuuming upstairs. You do get underfoot these days."

She was plainspoken and treated him like a cross between an older brother and the senile uncle everyone humored. It was his fault. When he hired her a year ago, he'd set the tone for their relationship, wanting—no, needing—someone in his life whom he could be himself around. That was part of why she'd crept beneath his skin. He didn't hold back around her. She was the one person who had heard all his darkest thoughts, his doubts, his secrets.

Except in one area: the way he'd come to feel about her.

And in turn, she'd talked to him about growing up in San Francisco and how she met her husband. Her eyes glowed when she talked about him and turned teary when she spoke of how Honey would grow up never knowing her father. Claire was not a woman who loved easily and then moved on.

How could he take advantage of someone like that? A single mother with no one to turn to if she lost both her job and the place she lived.

He might not be the best guy in the world—London could attest to that—but there were some lines he wouldn't cross. And seducing Claire was one of them.

Claire's heart ached as she watched Linc with Honey. The man was too ridiculously good-looking for her peace of mind. Since he broke off his engagement to London, it had become harder and harder to resist fantasizing about her and Honey being part of Linc's family. When the daydreams were at their strongest, she slid on her rubber gloves and cleaned his bathroom. Reminding herself that she was his housekeeper—not a beautiful, successful and pedigreed Charlestonian woman—grounded her flights of fancy. After all, Linc's mother, Bettina Thurston, had barely tolerated London, and the socialite had had it all: money, success and beauty.

Claire stared at Linc's bulging biceps as he lifted Honey high into the air and whirled her around until she shrieked in excitement. It was nearly impossible to deny the man's appeal when he made her child happy. Nor did it help that his strong jaw, laughter-filled blue eyes and sensual lower lip made her blood run hot. Most days she wished he acted the part of a self-absorbed, successful jerk who thought all women were there to satisfy him. Then she wouldn't have had any tingly feelings for him.

"What are your plans for today?" he asked, settling Honey against his chest.

Her baby patted his cheek with a chubby palm and cooed at him. But Linc's bright blue eyes remained focused on Claire and the steadiness of his gaze made her temperature rise. She wanted to fan herself and drawl, *Oh, my*. She'd felt that way a lot since the baseball season ended and he'd returned from Texas. Too often. She couldn't let this go on. There had to be some way to stop or at least slow her ever-increasing attraction to him.

Claire pictured his mother's reaction to her predicament and that worked pretty well to cool her fever. Bettina was a true Southern belle from an old family line and rarely missed an opportunity to mention it. Having a pedigree in this town wasn't synonymous with having money. Even though Bettina's family had lost much of their fortune in the 1930s, her social standing hadn't been lowered, which made it unrealistic that she would accept Claire as a suitable match for her son.

"Claire?" Linc's deep voice roused her from her thoughts.

"I'm sorry. I was thinking about all the things I have to do today."

"What if I take Lil' Bit here off your hands, so you can get everything done faster and knock off early?" He tickled Honey, prompting a delighted giggle.

Claire shook her head. It wasn't professional to let her boss play nanny, but in the months she'd worked for Linc, the line had grown ever more blurry between employer and friend.

"You don't have to do that," she said. "I can take care of everything."

Yet the way the pair got along, it was tempting to surrender Honey to Linc's care. And Claire had other concerns. With Jasper dead, Honey was going to grow up without a father. Claire wanted her daughter to know a good man, but she couldn't let that be Linc. Plus, she worried that Honey would get attached to him in ways she shouldn't. What happened when Linc got married and started to have babies of his own? How confused would Honey be when his children took his full attention and he had no more time for her?

"I could use the company," Linc continued.

Curse the man for being so persistent.

Claire opened her mouth to refuse yet again, but something in his manner stopped her. Since breaking off his engagement to the incredibly beautiful and successful London, his behavior had changed. It was as if he'd lost a bit of his cockiness, which was strange, since she knew he was the one who'd ended things. Maybe Linc had decided that had been a mistake.

London had already rebounded, making a splash in the society pages after being seen on the arm of millionaire playboy and race car driver Harrison Crosby. Claire wouldn't be surprised if Linc was a little jealous that London had bounced back so fast.

"You can't watch Honey," Claire said, plucking her daughter from his grasp.

Honey protested being taken away from Linc, but

Claire struggled to maintain a severe expression while ignoring her daughter's scowl. It was like trying not to smile at a puppy growling fiercely as it plays. Honestly, the child was too adorable for her own good. She'd inherited her father's charisma. The man could charm fruit off trees. Or the pants off unsuspecting culinary school students, which was what she'd been when they first met.

"If I remember correctly," Claire continued, "you're supposed to have lunch with your mother today."

Linc made a face. "I haven't forgotten."

He grabbed his duffel bag and turned to leave the kitchen. Before he took more than two steps, Claire cleared her throat. When he pivoted back around, she was holding up the smoothie. Disgust twisted his handsome features, but he took the drink. She didn't know what sorts of things he put into his body when he was away from Charleston, but while he was within her care, she made sure he ate nutritious and delectable meals.

"I want to see you taste it before you leave," she said. "That way I know you won't throw it out."

"You seem pretty sure of yourself." He lifted the glass and took a doubtful sniff.

"Food can be healthy and delicious."

"In my experience, the two don't go hand in hand." He radiated suspicion as he took a small sip. "Hey!" His eyes widened. "This one actually tastes good."

Her heart did a happy little leap. To cover her reaction to his praise, she gave a satisfied nod. "I added a little agave syrup to satisfy your sweet tooth."

"You're the best."

Warmed by his words, Claire let her gaze linger on his departing figure. Then shaking herself free of his spell, she carried her daughter into the sunroom next to the kitchen, where Honey had stripped off her clothes earlier. The room was filled with books and toys to keep the toddler occupied while Claire worked in the kitchen.

Once Honey was dressed, Claire settled her into a booster chair at the kitchen table. Sunlight spilled across the two-year-old's light brown hair, awakening the gold highlights and making her hazel eyes twinkle. She had her father's coloring. Claire's espresso hair and brown eyes were not at all represented. The only mark she'd made on her daughter was her petite frame. Where Jasper had been six-three and broadly built, Honey was in the twenty-fifth percentile for height and weight.

With Linc off to the gym, the house settled back into its usual state of harmonious calm. It wasn't that his energy was all that chaotic, but his presence tended to stir up feelings Claire would have preferred not to think about. Plus, during the seven months of baseball season, she'd grown accustomed to having the four-bedroom, five-bathroom home in the prestigious South of Broad— or SOB—neighborhood to herself and Honey.

While the toddler ate bits of a homemade blueberry waffle and slices of banana, Claire made out a grocery list. Linc had decided to host a dinner party on Saturday. It was his first time entertaining formally since his engagement to London had ended. When they were together, the socialite had preferred to host all their events at her mansion. London had always made it clear she doubted Claire's experience and sophistication to pull off a Charleston-worthy event. On the surface, London had been right to judge Claire this way. Her upbringing in San Francisco was a pretty far cry from the pomp and circumstance that ruled Charleston society.

But Claire cooked like a dream. Everyone who'd tasted her food said so. In fact, it was on the strength of her culinary skills that she'd found her way to filling in for Bettina's housekeeper during a ladies' luncheon and eventually taking the job with Linc.

As soon as Honey finished her breakfast, Claire dressed her in an adorable outfit she'd found at a consignment shop and headed to the local gourmet grocery store with her list. The menu required several specialty ingredients and Claire knew she'd find everything she needed there.

While she shopped, she kept Honey occupied by practicing her colors.

"What color is this?" Claire asked, showing her a box of elbow macaroni.

"Green," Honey crowed and clapped her hands, obviously pleased with herself.

"That's right. It's green." She gave her daughter a smoochy kiss on her cheek, making her giggle.

"Well, isn't she a bright little girl."

Claire turned toward the speaker, a stunning woman in her early thirties with bright green eyes and dark blond hair subtly highlighted with gold. She had perfect skin and full lips, and her flawless makeup softened the angles of her face. In a yellow T-shirt and a flowered skirt, Claire felt dowdy and uninteresting beside her.

"Thank you. She picks up things so very quickly,"

she said, her wide smile broadcasting her pride. "She's already counting to fifty and knows her ABCs."

"My goodness. How old is she?"

"She just turned two last month."

The woman looked suitably impressed. "You must work with her a great deal."

"I'm home with her all day, so that really makes a difference."

The woman's gaze flicked to the plain gold band on Claire's left hand. Her first inclination was to cover the betraying lack of sparkle. A part of Claire winced at the impulse. In this part of town, status was everything, and she'd grown tired of how fast she was dismissed. Claire pushed her irritation aside. She was a housekeeper. She shouldn't be worrying about anyone's perception of her. Still, it smarted a little every time she glimpsed disdain in someone's eyes.

But there was nothing but kind interest in the woman's expression. "I bet you read to her all the time."

"I do. She loves books." Claire beamed at Honey, realizing how many memories of her own childhood involved her mother reading to her in the overstuffed armchair in their living room. "Do you have any children?"

"No. I'm not married." The woman sighed. "As much as I love children, I'm not really sure I'm cut out for motherhood."

"It's not always easy."

The woman acknowledged the remark with a faint smile. "I'm Everly Briggs."

"Nice to meet you, Everly. I'm Claire Robbins and this is my daughter, Honey."

"Well, Claire, that's an interesting collection of ingredients you have there," she said, letting her gaze travel over the contents of Claire's shopping cart. "What are you making?"

Smiling, Claire ticked off the menu she'd fretted over for the better part of a week. "Scallops with potato pancakes and caviar sauce. Braised lamb shanks with vegetable puree. And seared bitter greens with roasted beets and spiced pecans. And for dessert, a pomegranate-chocolate cake."

With each menu item she listed, the woman's eyes grew wider. "Well, that's quite impressive. What's the occasion?"

"My employer is hosting a dinner party."

"Who might that be? I'll have to wrangle an invitation. It all sounds delicious."

Everly fired off the question so blithely that Claire answered before considering whether she should. "Lincoln Thurston."

The woman's friendly manner underwent a slight transformation at the mention of Linc's name. She stopped making polite conversation and became riveted. "Oh." Her smile took on a keen edge. "Now I really want to come to the party. I heard he's single these days."

"Ah…yes."

Wishing she'd kept her mouth shut, Claire gathered breath to make a courteous exit, but the stranger latched on to the shopping cart, preventing Claire from going anywhere.

"I'm having some friends over next week and would love to hire you to cater my party."

"I'd love to, but I can't. When I said I worked for Linc…" Claire cursed her earlier lapse. For a moment, she'd seen the admiration in the woman's eyes and it had felt amazing. "I'm not his caterer. I'm his housekeeper."

"The one who lives-in?" Everly asked, a smooth drawl sugarcoating her avid curiosity.

Claire frowned. "Yes." *What was this woman after?*

"Oh." Everly shaded the word in all sorts of understanding. "Then you're the woman all Charleston is gossiping about."

Two

When Linc returned home from the gym, Claire's car wasn't in the driveway. She'd finalized the menu for his dinner party the night before and was likely shopping for ingredients. He was excited to have her cooking for his friends. Her culinary skills were fantastic. In fact, he was surprised she hadn't gone to work for a restaurant when she'd first moved to Charleston.

He'd asked her about it once and she'd explained about the long hours and how she'd struggled finding childcare. As he'd listened to her talk about her challenges being a single mom, he appreciated that she wanted to put her daughter's needs first. Still, he sensed there was more to the story. She seemed to lack confidence in her ability. Which made no sense. She cooked like a dream.

Maybe he'd put too much pressure on her. This was the first time he'd entertained since moving into the Battery Street house. While he and London had been together, she'd insisted on hosting all events. At first, he'd agreed because the house he'd purchased had gone through almost three years of renovations and wasn't the ideal place to entertain. But once the home had been restored to its former glory, his fiancée had been unable to relinquish control. Linc had begun to see their relationship wasn't the give-and-take partnership he craved. Too bad he hadn't realized this before proposing marriage.

Linc set his gym bag on a bar stool and rummaged in the refrigerator for something that would take the edge off his post-workout appetite. Claire always had snacks ready for him. Today was no exception. A quick glance at the clock confirmed that he had only an hour before his mother expected him for lunch. He was running late thanks to an impromptu shopping detour he'd made on the way to the gym. It had occurred to him as he was leaving the house that Claire had been working for him for a year. He'd neglected to mark the anniversary last week and decided to rectify the error. A few doors down from the gym was a boutique run by Theresa Owens, a friend of his sister Sawyer's from high school. He'd popped in to buy a small token.

After polishing off a turkey and Swiss cheese sandwich and a bowl of mixed berries, Linc rummaged for a pen to sign the card that would accompany the whimsical asymmetrical silver earrings embellished with turquoise, tourmaline and opal. He'd chosen earrings because aside from her plain wedding band, earrings were the only accessories he'd ever seen Claire wear.

Was it weird that he had bought Claire such a personal gift? He'd considered cash or a gift card but liked the idea of something he'd put thought into. Jewelry was a natural go-to purchase for him. His mother and sister both loved receiving sparkly earrings and necklaces. When he was a kid, there'd been little money available for such things. It made him feel good to be able to spoil the women in his life. And he knew they appreciated it.

Linc left the card and the jewelry box on the breakfast bar where Claire was sure to find them and headed upstairs to shower and change. His mother expected him to arrive at her house promptly at noon, wearing pressed trousers, a crisp shirt and a blazer. Money might have been in short supply while his mother had been young, but her upbringing had been rich in Southern custom.

Linc's grandmother had clung to memories of wealth and power long after her husband had sold their South of Broad home to a wealthy gentleman from "off"—a man who had no history in the city. Keeping up with private school tuition and social pressures, as well as the increased expense of maintaining the large historic houses, had meant difficult choices for many old Charleston families.

Yet, despite the downturn in his financial circumstances, Linc's grandfather had retained enough status to keep his family afloat socially. Linc's mother had never given up her dream of returning her family to its former glory, not even when her husband proved no more financially astute than her father had been, and his embezzlement scheme caused the government to seize their property and bank accounts.

That was why as soon as he signed his first pro contract, Linc had made sure to set his mother up in the sort of Charleston house that would provide Bettina the level of comfort her mother had known growing up. The Mills-Forrest House was located on King Street, South of Broad. Built in 1790, it had been extensively restored and renovated by Knox Smith to provide Bettina with the best blend of historic charm and modern function.

Knox was Linc's best friend. A real estate developer, he'd worked hard on transforming the city of Charleston to its former glory. During their twenties, the two bachelors had spent a significant amount of time tearing up the town and breaking hearts. They'd been quite the dynamic duo.

Twenty minutes later, as he entered his mother's parlor, Linc was once again struck by a wave of gratitude that he could do this for her. She was in her element, holding court from a comfortable chintz armchair by the fireplace.

"Good afternoon, Mother. You look splendid today." Linc crossed the room and bent down to kiss Bettina's soft cheek.

He lingered a second and inhaled her rose perfume, smiling at the memory of snuggling on her lap when he was young. Even after his sister came along and monopolized their mother's time, Bettina always made sure she hugged her son before he went to bed.

"Of course I look splendid," his mother shot back

tartly, her eyes twinkling. "I had a facial yesterday that took ten years off."

She squeezed his hand and then indicated the chair beside the sofa where she sat. On the side table was a silver bell. She picked it up and gave it a vigorous ring. A thin woman with gray-streaked blond hair appeared at the parlor door.

Dolly had been with his mother for ten years and the two women had developed a snarky, passive-aggressive relationship that worked for them. As outwardly hostile as his mother was toward the housekeeper, Linc was certain Bettina secretly enjoyed the ongoing battle. In turn, Dolly wasn't without a spine and often gave as good as she got. Linc didn't understand why she stayed. Dolly could have found less stressful employment in a dozen homes.

"Linc needs a martini," his mother proclaimed.

"No, thank you. Just some sparkling water with a lime." He bit down on the admonition that it was too early to start drinking, knowing his mother would simply ignore him.

"I'll have a bourbon with ice. Make sure you use the good stuff." Before Dolly was out of earshot, Bettina turned to Linc. "She's been giving me some swill she claims is from Grady's distillery. As if I haven't been drinking bourbon all my life and wouldn't know the difference."

Grady was Linc's cousin on his mother's side. Now that bourbon had been "rediscovered" by the masses, the trend seemed to be everyone with a little pocket change slapping a label on a barrel and calling it craft bourbon. Linc considered most of it swill. However, after attending one of Grady's tasting parties, Linc had been impressed enough to back his cousin's venture. So far, Grady hadn't gone bankrupt, so Linc figured his cousin must be doing something right.

"Tell me about your dinner party tomorrow night," Bettina said, turning her bright blue eyes on Linc. "Who all is invited?"

"The usual suspects. Knox, Sawyer, Austin, Roy, Grady and a few others. There will be twelve of us altogether."

His mother reeled back in dismay. "Did you invite any girls besides your sister?" Bettina had been unhappy when he started dating London and positively mortified when they got engaged. This time around he knew she intended to steer him toward a more appropriate choice, preferably a young woman whose Charlestonian roots went as deep as his own.

"She's promised to bring six friends so it'll be even numbers."

His mother had a knack for radiating displeasure without moving any of her facial muscles. "You can't let your love life be decided by your sister's random friends."

"I also can't let my love life be decided by my mother's social aspirations for me." He smiled to take any sting out of the words.

Bettina waved her hand as if she was shooing away a fly. "You have a duty to this family to marry well and have children who will carry on the Thurston name."

Seriously, Mother?

There was a time, after Linc's father was caught embezzling and went to jail for five years, that Bettina had cursed the Thurston name. Linc wisely chose not to point this out to her.

"If you don't ease up on my search parameters," Linc muttered, "I'm going to die childless and alone." He made it sound as if he was kidding, but in truth, he wasn't sure if he trusted himself to fall in love with the right woman.

Look at the mistake he'd made with London. He still wasn't clear if what he had felt for her was love, or if she'd simply won him over with her beauty, determined personality and competitive spirit.

They'd met when he was in his late twenties and starting to lose interest in the never-ending merry-go-round of women in and out of his life. He'd spotted her at a charity event she'd organized and been drawn to her beauty. That she'd also been blessed with brains and ambition had struck the right chord with him, and within a month, they'd become exclusive.

"Don't be ridiculous," his mother said. "I can name a dozen women who would be perfect for you. In fact, as soon as you leave, I'm going to make a list and invite them to a party here in a couple weeks. That girl of yours is a dream…"

While his mother prattled on, Linc grappled with his discomfort over being the main event at one of Bettina's gatherings. Part of him wanted to make his mother happy after everything she'd endured in her life, but he wasn't about to surrender his freedom unless the woman was nothing short of spectacular.

"…Claire?"

His heart gave a little jump as his mother mentioned the young widow. "What about Claire?" Had she guessed his ever-increasing preoccupation with the woman who worked for him?

"Can I borrow her to cater the party?"

His mother's request reminded Linc that his attraction to Claire needed to end. In any other town they could make it work, but in Charleston, where his mother was so entrenched in her family history, a Thurston and an outsider could never happen. Especially when that outsider was also his housekeeper.

"I'll ask her if she's willing," he said, his tone subdued.

"Wonderful. Send her by early next week so we can discuss the menu."

To Linc's relief, Dolly announced lunch a few minutes later. He could tell that the wheels were spinning in his mother's head. As the food was being served, Bettina demanded pen and paper so she could write down the list of appropriate women she intended to introduce to him.

Linc sipped tomato bisque soup and devoured curried shrimp and egg salad sandwiches in silence while his mother remarked over each woman she intended to include. Bettina made it sound as if they were candidates for him to choose from, but he knew the truth: the party would be one big husband hunt, with him, the unlucky prey.

The situation wasn't unfamiliar. Since high school, women had been throwing themselves at him. And once he'd started playing pro baseball, he couldn't turn around without a beautiful woman hitting on him. But those women weren't usually of a sort he took seriously. After a one-night stand or a brief hookup, they drifted out of his life.

This was different. His mother intended to toss him into a pit with a voracious group of marriage-minded females. He doubted he'd come out intact.

So Linc started making his own list of eligible guy friends whom he could persuade to attend to take some of the focus off him. He knew twenty who fit the bill, but the question remained: How many could he convince to attend? They had to realize what his mother was up to.

Over dessert, his mother turned her attention to gossiping about her neighbors and the antics of her former in-laws. There was little new or surprising in what she had to impart, and Linc let the white noise of her voice flow over him while he wondered if Claire had found the earrings and if she liked them.

The unique asymmetrical style wouldn't have suited most of the women he knew, but Claire would appreciate them. She had a quirky Bohemian style, a product of her growing up in California. He hoped she liked the interesting shapes and blue-green color of the stones. Would she guess that remembering turquoise was her favorite color had prompted him to choose this particular pair? Doubtful. He'd been doing a good job hiding his interest in her.

"I'm thinking about getting remarried." His mother's abrupt declaration jolted Linc out of his musings.

"Remarried?" he echoed dumbly, his thoughts scrambling to catch up. "I didn't realize you were seeing anyone."

"I'm not. At least, not exclusively."

Linc frowned. What did that mean? He narrowed his eyes and focused all his attention on his mother. "So you're seeing several men?"

He couldn't reconcile this with his mother's behavior after her husband went to jail, was released and then abruptly filed for divorce. After years of devoted support, Bettina had been blindsided, causing Linc to sever all contact with his father. Ever since, she'd kept a low profile and hadn't really dated, at least as far as Linc knew.

"Not in the way you're implying." His mother's tone sharpened. "I entertain gentlemen from time to time. They come by for lunch or cocktails. Sometimes dinner."

"Where do you meet these men?"

Bettina preened, obviously appreciating her son's alarm. "Is that concern I hear in your voice?"

"Of course it's concern. You can't just drop something like this on me." Linc shook his head. Today's lunch was certainly eventful. "Are you sure they're interested in you and not just—"

"I suggest you don't finish that statement," his mother said, eyes narrowing. "I'm an attractive woman."

"Yes, you are," he murmured.

Bettina rolled on as if he hadn't spoken. "With needs."

"Please, no more," he begged, cringing away from thoughts of his mother having any sort of sex life.

Bettina continued, either oblivious to or not concerned about her son's sensibilities. "You've been so busy with your life that you haven't paid all that much attention to what's going on with me or your sister." His mother paused for a beat. "Did you know she's been seeing someone?"

Linc shook his head, struck dumb by the twists and turns the conversation was taking. "Anyone I know?"

Bettina shook her head. "You know she doesn't tell me anything about her personal life."

Sawyer had learned that lesson watching their mother meddle in his life.

"Then how do you know?" he asked.

"A mother knows when her children are up to something, and Sawyer is definitely acting like she has a secret."

As the implication of Bettina's words hung in the air, Linc hoped that wasn't true, because the last thing he needed was for his mother to find out about his feelings for Claire.

Claire stood in the middle of The Market on Market and gaped at the woman who'd just issued such a provocative statement. With her brain short-circuited as the implications sank in, her entire body remained frozen. But as she watched Everly's gaze flick to Honey and narrow as if assessing the toddler from a fresh perspective, Claire regained her wits.

"Me?" she burst out, half laughing, half in irritation. "And Linc Thurston? That's absolutely ridiculous."

While Claire wasn't surprised the woman knew all

about Linc's severed relationship with London, she was stunned to be thought of as the reason for the breakup.

Everly's perfectly arched eyebrows rose. "Is it?"

"You have it all wrong. I'm his housekeeper." Not to mention she was the furthest thing from Linc's type.

He was attracted to beautiful, elegant women with money and social graces. A man of his wealth and social position needed an accomplished hostess at his side, someone of equal standing in Charleston. His mother would demand nothing less.

"You think it's unusual for a man to have an affair with his hired help?" Everly asked, her voice sly and full of salacious undertones.

Claire considered all the scandals that had arisen surrounding famous men and their female staff. From nannies to assistants to housekeepers. She supposed it made sense for the woman to jump to the wrong conclusion about her.

"Linc is not like that," she said with mounting dismay.

Why was she bothering to defend herself and Linc when this woman was so far off track, not to mention completely out of line?

"You're female. And you're pretty. I'm sure you can understand how it looks."

The woman's insistence made Claire ponder her interactions with Linc. Sure, they had an occasional flirtatious exchange, such as the one this morning about her skinny-dipping in his pool. Sudden heat flooded Claire's cheeks as she thought about how it could've been misinterpreted.

"He's never been anything but professional with me."

"Of course." But Everly didn't sound at all convinced.

Claire was on the verge of letting it go when she remembered that in Charleston's tight community even a whiff of scandal could be damaging. She sucked in a breath for one final clarification.

"Linc is surrounded by beautiful, interesting women all the time," Claire said evenly, keeping her features composed as she hit the woman with a final double-barreled shot. "I clean his toilets. There's nothing beautiful or interesting about that." Then, barely giving the woman a chance to let that sink in, she added, "Now, if you'll excuse me, I need to finish my shopping."

Claire pushed the cart forward. To her dismay, the woman wasn't giving up. Everly's heels clicked on the tile floor as she moved to intercept Claire once again. She snagged the shopping cart with one manicured hand and Claire noticed how she appeared contrite.

"I'm sorry. I was out of line to say what I did. Let me take you to lunch to apologize."

The urge to laugh almost overpowered Claire. She imagined how out of place she and Honey would be sitting down to a meal with Everly in one of the sophisticated restaurants that the elegant woman no doubt frequented.

"You don't need to do that."

"I feel terrible. Let me make it up to you."

The whiplash of the woman's abrupt turnaround left Claire feeling off balance. "I don't think so."

"Let me give you my card. You can call me when you have some free time."

With Everly's business card burning in her pocket, Claire finished her shopping. It had been easier to accept the card and agree to call the attractive blonde woman than to continue to put her off.

Anxiety had eased its grip on Claire once she got in line to pay for her groceries. Really, it was almost funny that anyone could imagine she was attractive enough to catch Linc's attention. The idea was absurd. By the time Claire exited the grocery store, with a small bag of items on one hip and her daughter on the other, she'd chalked up her encounter with Everly to one of the pitfalls of working for someone in the public eye.

Claire stored the groceries in her trunk before settling Honey into her safety seat in the back seat of her ten-year-old gray Saab. The car had taken her from California to Charleston when she fled with her daughter after Jasper's parents started threatening her with a custody suit. To obscure her trail and make it hard for them to know where she'd gone, Claire had sold her former car and paid cash for the Saab. A friend had helped by registering the car in his name. Claire probably should've ditched the Saab when she reached Charleston, but she felt unaccountably secure after she reached the city.

In an odd way, when she'd exited I-26 and driven south on Market Street all the way into historic downtown Charleston, she'd been overwhelmed by a sense of coming home. Which was ridiculous, because until a little over a year ago, the farthest east she'd ever been was Las Vegas.

During the short drive back to Linc's house, she

shook off the eerie feeling from the odd encounter with Everly. In a town like Charleston, it made sense that most people would feel as if they had some connection to Linc and speculate on the reason behind his abrupt breakup with London.

He was a media darling. Not only was he a famous baseball player, handsome, wealthy and from one of Charleston's older families, but he was also an active philanthropist, offering his personal and financial support to numerous charities. His innate charisma dominated whatever room he walked into. In short, Linc was a colossal celebrity.

"People make up all sorts of absurd things," she remarked to her daughter as she unbuckled Honey from her seat and lifted her out.

As soon as Honey's sandal-covered feet touched the brick pavers of Linc's driveway, the toddler made a beeline for the kitchen door, leaving her mother to follow more slowly after collecting her bags. In addition to grocery shopping, Claire had purchased flowers and containers for centerpieces. She intended to make those up this afternoon because tomorrow would be reserved for cooking.

"Mama!" Honey's excited call pulled Claire away from the refrigerator, where she'd been putting food away.

"What, baby?"

Honey's bare feet slapped the kitchen's wood floor as she brought her mother a small flat box of a size perfect for earrings. "Blue."

"Yes, it is. Where did you find that?"

Honey pointed to the center island. Claire glanced over and spied a white envelope. She took the present from her daughter's hand and carried it back to where Honey had found it. She set the box on the envelope and her daughter immediately protested.

"No!"

"That's not ours to play with."

"Mama." Another thing Honey had inherited from her father was stubbornness. The toddler marched back to the island, climbed up on the nearest chair and once again reached for the present. "Mine."

As quick as her daughter could be, Claire had learned to be quicker. She scooped up the envelope and present, depositing them into the upper cupboard that held everyday dishes. Honey set her hands on her hips and scowled her displeasure.

Lips twitching, Claire turned her back to her daughter and began making her lunch. It was almost one and her errands had taken longer than she'd expected. Not until Honey sat at the kitchen table with turkey, cheese and apple slices did the two-year-old's sour expression ease. With her daughter occupied, Claire focused on the centerpiece arrangements. During the two-year period in her life when she'd been attending culinary school, to make ends meet Claire had gone to work for a florist, first as a delivery driver and then as an arranger.

"Nice flowers," she heard Linc say from the back door.

Claire looked up from her project and spied him entering the kitchen. Her heart gave a foolish little jump. He looked handsome in his navy blazer with the delphinium-blue pocket square that matched his eyes.

"Thank you, but the arrangement is far from done."

"I like the colors you picked out." He approached the center island where she was working and selected a stem of pale gold freesia. Setting the horn-shaped flowers to his nose, he inhaled. "This one smells good."

"I thought the color and shape would go nice with the Golden Forest china. What do you think?"

Although Claire doubted Linc cared which of his three sets of dishes she chose, talking—or babbling, in this case—kept her from doing something foolish, like blurting out the story of her encounter with Everly.

"And the Waterford, of course," she continued. "Your mother would approve. What do you think?"

She clamped her lips together to shut down the flow of words, all too aware that Linc was eyeing her. Damn that woman in the grocery store for filling her head with thoughts of being in a steamy affair with Linc.

"Sounds like you have everything in hand." He glanced at the spot where Honey had found the jewelry box and envelope and then surveyed the rest of the kitchen.

When his brows drew together, Claire realized what he must be looking for. "I put it in the cabinet," she explained, wiping her hands on a dish towel before crossing to where she'd secured the present. "Honey was all over it. We've been working on her colors and she noticed the box was blue."

"Blue," Honey chortled from the kitchen table, clapping her hands enthusiastically. "Mama. Down."

"Finish your lunch, baby." Claire retrieved the box and envelope and extended it to Linc.

"You didn't open it?" he asked in surprise.

"No." Claire gave her head a vigorous shake. She'd never step across the line like that. Was that what he'd made of her bout of awkward chattiness earlier? That she'd snooped and felt guilty about it? She placed the gift on the counter in front of him and returned to her flower arranging. "I'd never do something like that."

"Mama. Down."

A weird buzzing filled Claire's ears, distorting her daughter's voice, as a lazy smile played over Linc's lips. He set his hand on the counter and leaned in her direction.

"Did you even look at the envelope?"

A lock of blond hair fell across his forehead, lending a boyish charm to his already overwhelming handsomeness. She realized his effect on her had grown stronger lately.

What would it be like to have him close his arms around her and kiss her hard and deep? Just the thought of being crushed between his ripped body and the unyielding kitchen cabinets made her blood heat. She reflexively clamped down on the rose stem she was holding and winced as a thorn pricked her thumb.

"No," she said, sticking the injured thumb in her mouth. "Should I have?"

"Mama!" Honey was rocking in her booster seat, demanding that Claire release her.

"It's for you."

Her stomach dropped to her toes at his sly grin. He'd

bought her a gift? Why would he have done that? From his triumphant expression, he was obviously pleased with himself. Despite her lingering discomfort from Everly's scandalous assumptions, Claire found herself smiling back at Linc with no clear understanding why.

"For me?" In her bewilderment, she sounded like a complete chowderhead.

"Your name is on the envelope, isn't it?"

"It is?" Her pulse jerked in an erratic rhythm as she shifted her gaze to the small box and envelope.

He tapped the center of the paper where *Claire* was scrawled in Linc's familiar handwriting. "It is."

"I don't understand." The jewelry box felt heavy in her hand.

"You've been working for me for a year. I bought you something to celebrate your anniversary."

"You didn't have to do that." But she was thrilled that he had and more than a little relieved that was all there was to it.

She'd enjoyed working for him this past year. His house had become her sanctuary and she'd do anything to protect that. Feeling safe was a luxury she hadn't known since she'd become pregnant with Honey.

"I wanted to." His deep voice resonated through her. "Why don't you take a look at what I got you. I've been dying to see if you like it."

Something in his tone made her skin flush hot.

"Of course I'll like it." Telling herself it was silly to feel so breathless over an anniversary token didn't stop the flutters in her stomach. "You have wonderful taste."

Linc was always doing something nice for the women

in his life. His mother loved to collect cloisonné pill-boxes, so he was always on the lookout for them. And whenever he visited her house, he never showed up empty-handed. It might be a bouquet of flowers, sugar-glazed pecans or a bottle of craft bourbon—Linc was always thinking of what Bettina might enjoy.

He'd been the same way with London. In her case, his purchases had been expensive pieces of jewelry or designer handbags. His sister liked gadgets, so when-ever Linc ran across something new and innovative, he made sure Sawyer got one.

Conscious of Linc's keen blue eyes on her, Claire started with the card. As she glanced at the cover, some of the tightness in her throat eased. He'd chosen some-thing funny, a drawing of a dog wearing a big smile above the words *Thank You*. But when she flipped open the card and glanced at what he'd written, tears stung her eyes.

You've been a bright spot in my life for the last year. Thanks for all you've done. —Linc

"That's so nice," Claire croaked out, blinking rap-idly to clear her vision. "Honey and I have really ap-preciated how kind and generous you've been. Not to mention patient." She indicated the kitchen table, where her daughter was throwing herself back and forth in the chair and chanting to get down.

"It's been great having you here." He went over to lift Honey into his arms. "Both of you."

Claire refused to give in to the warmth suffusing her

For a span of a few heartbeats, Claire seemed to stop breathing. Had it been too much that he'd not only remembered her favorite color, but also that he'd found her something quirky to match her style?

"I've never seen anything like these," she murmured.

"I got them at that boutique Sawyer's friend owns. A local artist makes them. Each pair is one of a kind. I thought you'd appreciate that."

"I do." A smile accompanied her words, but it lacked something, making Linc frown.

"You're sure you like them? I have the receipt if you want to return them and choose something else." Hopefully she wouldn't. He wanted her to wear something he'd picked out for her.

"I'd never do that," she rushed to assure him. "They're beautiful and I'll treasure them." As if to indicate the conversation was at an end, she set the top back on the box and put it aside. "Thank you."

Linc wondered if the earrings were destined for a drawer, never to see the light of day again. His mood dipped. This wasn't at all the outcome he'd been hoping for. He wanted her to love the earrings and think of him every time she wore them. Each time they tickled her neck, he'd imagine the contact was his lips grazing across her soft, fragrant skin. If he couldn't touch her, he wanted something from him to caress her.

"You're not going to wear them?" He couldn't stop himself from asking the question.

She shook her head. "They're too fancy for every day."

"Then you'll wear them tonight when I take you and Honey out for dinner."

She looked appalled. "Dinner? Tonight?"

"Part two of your anniversary celebration."

"But I have so much to do to get ready for tomorrow night's dinner party." She gestured to the flowers. "Why don't I make something and we can eat here."

"I don't want you cooking or cleaning up." He assumed she'd appreciate eating a meal she hadn't prepared. "Let me give you a break from all that. A thank-you for all you've done for me."

Her mouth opened and closed as if she wanted to continue arguing. At last, she nodded. "May I pick the place?"

"Of course. Where would you like to go?"

"There's a seafood restaurant by Wappoo Creek I've been dying to try."

"If it's seafood you want, the yacht club has a fantastic restaurant."

When her eyes widened in dismay, Linc wondered what was wrong.

"I'd really rather not go there." Her chin lifted and her body language screamed determination. "And you said I could choose wherever I wanted." When he nodded, she relaxed. "Besides, I'd rather go somewhere more kid-friendly, since Honey is coming along."

"There are always families eating at the yacht club. You don't need to worry about Honey being out of place."

She shook her head. "How was lunch with your mother?"

Her change of subject reminded him of his mother's request. He grimaced.

"She wants to throw a party and asked if you could cater it."

"Of course." Even as she spoke, her gaze grew unfocused. The wheels were already turning as she sorted through what treats she might prepare. "When is the party?"

"Two weeks."

Another woman might have protested, but Claire merely nodded. "What's the occasion?"

"Nothing special." No need to explain that his mother intended to throw him to the wolves. "She just wants to invite some friends over."

"Did she mention how many people?"

"Not really." He sounded positively grim.

Claire gave him a curious once-over before saying, "I'll give her a call and discuss the particulars."

"If it gets to be too much, let me know. I don't want you feeling overwhelmed."

"Don't worry." She dismissed his concern with a flick of her hand. "Steve and Jenny will be here for your party tomorrow. I'll ask them if they're available. It's a little last-minute, but if they're busy, I'm sure they'll know some other people who could help serve." Claire glanced at the flowers on the counter. "Now, I'd better get back to these. I have lots to do before tomorrow night."

"Dinner at six?" Linc proposed, naming an earlier time than he usually ate so they could have a leisurely meal and still get home for Honey's bedtime.

"Sure. That will be fine."

Nodding, Linc headed for the stairs. With a packed

schedule from February to October, he should have appreciated the downtime during off-season. Instead, he chafed at the inactivity. It gave him too much time to think.

Lately, he'd been preoccupied with life after baseball. He'd had a great run, but he was going to be thirty-four when his contract was up. Despite the fact that his performance hadn't slowed, at that age, there was no way he would get another big deal. Nor was he even sure he'd still be playing for the Barons. How much longer did he think his career in the major leagues was going to last?

So what was he planning to spend the rest of his life doing? It wasn't as if he needed the money. Even after taking care of his mother and sister, funding the charities he worked with, and buying and restoring his house, he'd spent only a small percentage of his millions. Most of the money went into investments that would sustain him long past his contract's end.

What he needed was to find something that inspired him. Because when baseball no longer consumed his life, he was going to go crazy. He envied Knox's passion for restoring Charleston's historic properties and his love of sailing, both locally and all over the world. Linc had joined Knox on several adventures but preferred a spacious suite on land to the claustrophobic quarters of a sailboat.

Knox's face appeared on the screen of Linc's phone, as if his thoughts had summoned his friend. He answered the call.

"What's up?"

"My afternoon appointment canceled," Knox said,

sounding chipper. "Want to hit the batting cages so I can give you a few tips? Maybe you can bring your average up next season."

Linc grunted good-naturedly as he took the hit. He'd been in a slump for the last four weeks of the season. All the sports commentators pointed to his broken engagement as the reason, but that had been the cure, not the cause of his problem.

"Sure," he said. "I need to change. Meet you in thirty?"

"See you then."

An hour later, as he took his turn with the pitching machine, Linc felt some of his tension melt away. Playing baseball had always let him escape whatever troubled him. It had been a godsend when his father went to jail and then divorced Bettina, abandoning the three of them to start a new life. Sometimes Linc wondered if he would have been good enough to make it in the majors if he hadn't practiced so much back then.

He'd devoted every spare second to batting practice and perfecting his fielding techniques. Granted, he'd been endowed with a great deal of natural talent as well, but mostly he attributed his success to hard work and determination.

"Want to grab a beer after this?" Knox asked as they exchanged places.

"Can't."

Knox shot him a look. "Got plans?"

"I'm having dinner…" Linc paused, gripped by a sudden reluctance to tell his best friend about the anniversary dinner with Claire. He didn't want to hear

Knox's opinion on taking the beautiful widowed house-keeper and her adorable toddler out to dinner.

"Anyone I know?" Knox quizzed, his tone sly.

"It's not like that," Linc countered. As much as he hated keeping Knox in the dark, Linc didn't want to get into a huge discussion about Claire. Deciding a subject change was in order, he steered his best friend on to the topic he loved best. "How's the King Street project coming along? Have you got the plans approved yet?"

Six months ago Knox had purchased a building in the heart of the business district and was in the process of getting the permits to turn it into a ten-unit luxury condo complex. He'd paid four million for the property, and at the moment it was occupied by college students.

Working with their friend Austin's architectural firm, he'd commissioned plans that would include two private roof decks, as well as amenity space that would hold up to forty-eight people in the rear. Built in 1947, the building wasn't a historic property, but the location offered an opportunity for people to buy in the down-town area and that was always a draw.

"Not yet. The BAR requested we tweak a couple things on the rooftop decks before they'd give the go-ahead." The Board of Architecture Review met only twice a month, so the approval process was never speedy. "We're slotted into the agenda for next week, so hopefully the third time's the charm."

Knox didn't sound particularly stressed about the de-lays. They were the norm when doing any construction or development in the old city and the historic district. In fact, as frustrating as the board could be as they scrutinized projects from a dozen different angles, Linc knew Knox appreciated the board's dedication to preserving Charleston's past.

Of course, there was the other, less sentimental motivation for keeping the romance of Charleston's historic district alive: tourism. The city survived on its five million visitors each year who brought in nearly four billion dollars in revenue. And the number-one reason cited for visiting Charleston was the city's history and historic sites, followed by restaurants and local cuisine.

"I hope you get the approval this time around," Linc said.

Knox nodded. "Are you still planning on making the hunting trip?" Knox's family owned a large plantation a couple hours west of Charleston. Each fall, Knox brought a handful of his friends there for a weekend of deer hunting.

Linc cursed. Until now, he hadn't realized that the hunting trip and his mother's party were happening at the same time.

"I'm going to have to skip it this year. My mom's decided to host a party and wants me to attend."

"Can't you tell her you already have plans?"

"Not exactly." Linc was starting to understand how the deer must feel as Knox's buddies gathered for their weekend of sport. "I'm afraid the party is about finding someone for me to date."

"I'm not surprised," Knox said with a broad grin. "She wasn't too happy when you picked London. I'm sure she'll make sure every woman there will be perfect for you."

"Their pedigrees will be everything she could ever ask for," Linc replied. "As for whether they'll be perfect for me…that remains to be seen."

Claire noticed a slight tremble in her hands as she dressed Honey in a new outfit to go out to dinner with Linc. Excitement raced through her body, bringing a sparkle to her eyes and color to her cheeks. She'd noticed the betraying effect while applying eyeliner and sweeping brick-red gloss across her smiling lips. It was impossible to subdue her high spirits despite several reproachful warnings to herself.

This was just a casual dinner between a boss and employee to celebrate one year of employment. Common enough in a professional setting. Nothing to get giddy over. Yet scolding herself didn't settle her jittery nerves. Feeling this way would only bring her trouble. Plain and simple, she found her boss attractive, and instead of shutting her emotions down, she reveled in the thought that they were going to spend the evening together.

Fight it though she might, Claire had always been led by her emotions. If she'd done a better job listening to logic, she might have avoided getting involved with Jasper. On the other hand, whatever mistakes she'd made with him had given her Honey, and she wouldn't trade her daughter for anything. Still, in the past few years, she'd become more cautious when following her heart.

"There," she told her daughter, stepping back to admire the pale blue sundress covered in bright butterflies she'd recently bought. "You look so nice."

A quick glance at the clock showed they were running late. Claire twisted her daughter's hair into a loose topknot and fastened a bow. She felt a twinge at how adorable the two-year-old looked. Honey's hair had the perfect length and texture to do all sorts of fun braids and updos, and when Claire had time, she enjoyed experimenting with ideas she gleaned off the internet.

"Can you play with your toys for a couple minutes while Mama gets dressed?"

Honey nodded and headed toward the books that lined the lower shelf of the nightstand in her room.

Claire headed next door to slip into the dress she had laid out. It was a simple short-sleeved dress, the color of wisteria. She fit her feet into a pair of beige sandals and snagged a white sweater out of her closet in case she needed it.

In less than five minutes, she returned to her daughter's room to collect Honey, and the two of them headed downstairs.

Linc awaited them in the kitchen. He wore khaki pants and a navy cotton sweater over a white button-down shirt. The look was perfect for the casual seafood restaurant near Wappoo Creek.

"Oh, good," he said, "you both have sweaters. I reserved a table outside. I thought you might enjoy the view."

"That sounds wonderful."

Linc escorted them out to his car. Earlier he'd borrowed her keys so he could transfer Honey's car seat from Claire's Saab into the back of his white BMW X6. As she slid into the passenger seat, Claire couldn't help but savor the thrill of being enfolded in the soft camel leather. The Saab was in good shape, but it couldn't compare to this sort of luxury.

"All set?" Linc asked, glancing at Claire.

She nodded. As they made their way west on Broad Street, her anxiety began to fade. She and Linc had dined together several times in the year she'd been working for him. Granted, all those times had been impromptu meals in the kitchen or out by the pool, but it wasn't like this was some momentous occasion. It was a work dinner.

"I've been thinking about the party my mom wants to have," he began, breaking the silence as they crossed the Ashley River. "I hope you don't feel obligated to do it."

"Of course not." While Linc was gone for the summer, Claire didn't have a lot to do and she had assisted Dolly with three of Bettina's dinner parties. "I'm always happy to help her out."

"It's extra work and, of course, you'll be compensated."

While she understood what he was getting at and appreciated his attempt to be fair, the conversation did serve to drive home that she worked for him. Maybe this was exactly what she needed to hear. A reminder of their relative positions. He was the boss. She, the employee. It cut the jubilant buzz about their evening nearly in half, so that by the time they reached the restaurant, she'd successfully tamed her wayward pulse.

Linc took charge of getting Honey out of her car seat and carrying her into the restaurant. Although the two-year-old was perfectly capable of walking, Linc always seemed to be in a hurry to get places and her short stubby legs were no match for his long ones.

The hostess led them to a table that overlooked the water. Although called a creek, the average width of the Wappoo was ninety feet. It connected the intracoastal waterways around Charleston. Beyond the weathered wooden railing extended a dock, where several small boats were tied.

Linc settled into his chair, looking completely at home in the casual atmosphere. "I didn't realize they had a dock," he said. "Next time we should come by boat." He noticed her looking at him and cocked an eyebrow. "What?"

"You look like you fit right in."

"Why shouldn't I?"

"This place is a little more casual than what I imagine you're used to."

"You forget I didn't always have money. In fact, I waited tables at a place very much like this the summer before my senior year of high school."

"I have a hard time picturing you waiting tables."

"Why?"

She was used to thinking about him as someone she took care of. It was hard to imagine him taking orders and schlepping food.

"You don't really seem the sort."

"The money was good." He paused and regarded her with a slight frown. "I know what it's like to struggle and worry about taking care of my family."

"I know." But she couldn't picture him as desperate or poor.

"I didn't go to private school. My mom worked hard to take care of Sawyer and me. When I got old enough to pitch in and help, I did." As he spoke, his gaze grew more piercing. "So you see, we're not so different. If I hadn't been good enough to make it in the majors, our paths might've crossed in a restaurant instead." He frowned thoughtfully.

While she wondered what had prompted his change in mood, a waiter approached to take their drink order. When she ordered a lemonade, Linc shook his head.

"What about a glass of wine?" he prompted. "We're celebrating, remember?"

She wasn't sure alcohol was a good idea but didn't want to disappoint him. "What are you having?"

"I'm going to have a beer."

"Make it two." She turned her attention to the menu. "This all looks delicious."

"Is there anything in particular you had in mind?"

"They're known for their steampots," she pointed out, noting there were six to choose from.

"Let's get the Battery Street Bucket."

Naturally, he'd pick the most expensive dish on the menu. Her mouth watered as she scanned what all was included. In addition to shrimp and sausage, the pot contained both Alaskan snow and king crab as well as lobster. It was something she'd never have been able to afford, but since Linc insisted they were celebrating, Claire nodded.

"And how about a dozen raw oysters to start?" he prompted.

"Why not."

When the waiter returned with their drinks, Linc placed their order and Claire selected macaroni and cheese for Honey. Linc insisted they needed a side of hush puppies as well. She laughed as she contemplated how they were going to get through so much food.

"You must be hungry."

"I worked up an appetite at the batting cages with Knox this afternoon." Linc took a long pull from his beer and set the bottle down. "He seems to think that I need the practice because of my end-of-season slump."

"He should be nicer to you. Doesn't he realize you were under a lot of pressure this year because of what was going on in your personal life?"

Linc snorted. "No one cares."

"That's not fair."

"They're not paying me all those millions so I can let a failed romance distract me," he pointed out.

"I suppose not." She pushed her glass around the weathered table. "But you didn't have a failed romance," she countered, unsure where the compulsion to stick up for him was coming from. "You decided things weren't working. It wasn't anyone's fault. Sometimes love dies."

His gaze sharpened. "Are you speaking from experience?"

"Sure." Claire pondered her relationship with Jasper.

"So you were in love with someone before you met your husband?"

Recognizing her mistake, Claire said, "I guess I thought I was."

She hated lying to Linc about being married to Jasper but couldn't change her story a year into her deception. If only she'd thought the whole thing through before deciding life would be less complicated if everyone thought she was still grieving her hero husband. And the truth was, she had moments when she missed Jasper. Or at least the Jasper she'd fallen in love with. The one who'd been a gentle lover and romantic boyfriend.

"You guess?" Linc echoed, his expression curious.

"Sure. I mean, how much does anyone know about being in love when they're still in their teens?"

"How old were you when you met your husband?"

"I'd just turned twenty. It was Mother's Day. He'd come into the florist where I started working after high school, looking for a gift for his mom." She'd thought it was sweet the way he'd considered her opinion on the perfect bouquet.

"Did he sweep you off your feet?"

"No. I was dating someone. And Jasper was almost eight years older than me. That, combined with his military experience, made him seem too mature." Plus, at the time, he'd just gone through a horrendous divorce and wasn't in a place where he was interested in dating. He was more interested in getting Stephanie out of his system with a string of hookups.

"So, what changed?"

"My boyfriend at the time was an immature idiot." She smiled faintly, remembering the day she'd woken up to the fact that she wanted to date someone whose idea of fun went beyond partying and playing video games. "I realized that a man who knew what he wanted and went after it was way more appealing."

"And Jasper wanted you?"

Claire nodded. "He'd made it pretty clear from the start."

"So you fell in love."

Linc made it sound so simple, but Claire couldn't look back on that time without remembering how Jasper had grown edgier each time he came back from an overseas tour. The way he behaved had made her a little afraid to tell him she was pregnant. But once he learned he was going to become a father, he'd gone back to the man she'd first met and had given her hope that he would be able to overcome his PTSD.

"I did." And she had. At least, she'd been in love in the beginning. "It happened pretty fast. Sometimes I think that was due to the fact that he was going to Fort Benning for training in a few months."

"Did you get married before he left?"

"No, we hadn't been together that long and I was in culinary school." Nor had Claire been convinced that she wanted to be a military wife, traveling to wherever her husband was posted, worrying whenever he was deployed.

Suddenly Claire didn't want to talk about Jasper or spin any more half-truths about their relationship. She was overcome by relief as the waiter brought their appetizers and she focused on breaking up a hush puppy so it would cool down enough for Honey to be able to eat it. Several minutes went by before Claire shifted her attention back to Linc.

"I'm sorry if I made you uncomfortable with my questions about your husband," he said, squeezing lemon onto several of the oysters.

"You didn't."

"I don't think that's true."

His ability to read her made Claire wary. At least he didn't know why she was uncomfortable. "It must seem like I can't move on…"

"I can't imagine what it's like to lose someone you love like that." Linc doctored one of the oysters with horseradish and cocktail sauce before lifting the shell to his lips and letting it slide into his mouth. When he set the empty shell down, his eyes glinted with pleasure.

Claire followed his example and sighed in delight as the sharp bite of horseradish mingling with the richness of the oyster lingered on her tongue. "This is exactly what I imagined when I decided to move to Charleston. Dining on fresh seafood by the water."

"California has water and seafood. What brought you here?"

"Believe it or not, my great-great-grandfather is from Charleston. He left here ten years before the Civil War began and chased gold all the way to California."

"Did he have any luck?"

"A little. But there were nearly a hundred thousand people who descended on California in 1849 alone, and the chances of getting rich weren't all that high. In the end, he decided there was more money to be made in supporting the gold-seekers and married a widow nearly ten years his senior. Together, they ran her hotel business." Claire's lips twitched.

"What?" Linc prompted.

"It's been argued among my family that it might have been more of a gaming establishment or brothel than a hotel."

"You don't say."

"It's pretty scandalous, don't you think? Especially when the story goes that James Robbins came from an elite Charleston family." Claire laughed. "Of course, none of it's true about my great-great-grandfather's background. But it sure makes for a good story."

"What makes you think it's not true?"

"Did you miss the part where James was a scoundrel? He probably told people he was from a wealthy Charleston family so they'd take him seriously as a businessman. At the time, Charleston was one of the richest cities in the country."

"How do you know all this?"

"Grandma Sylvia kept diaries. She and her first husband traveled from Massachusetts in 1848. He died on the way, and when she got to California, she figured out that men coming out of the mountains with gold would want all the creature comforts they could afford."

"You know a lot about this."

"My great-aunt Libby was really into all this genealogy stuff. She was a women's studies professor at Berkeley."

"Did she ever look into James Robbins of Charleston?"

"I don't know. Libby died five years ago."

"You should talk to Sawyer about this. Her friend Ruby likes to dig into old records. Maybe she could find some mention of James."

As a member of the preservation society, Sawyer would be a good resource for such a quest. "I wouldn't want to bother her."

"Are you kidding? One thing about this town is they love their history. I'll bet Ruby would enjoy hearing your story."

Although Claire knew Sawyer wasn't prone to gossip, she didn't want anyone to start poking around her background and discover that she wasn't a widow. The best thing would be to let the whole matter drop, but she knew Linc wouldn't understand why she wanted to do that. Abruptly, Claire wished she'd never said anything about her family.

"I'll give Sawyer a call," she said and hoped her promise would pacify him, because the last thing she needed was for Jasper's parents to find her in Charleston.

Four

Dinner wasn't going quite the way Linc had hoped. Claire had become subdued and distracted after talking about her husband. He'd intended for the evening to be fun and entertaining. Instead, he'd dredged up her past and reminded her of all she'd lost.

How terrifying it must have been for her to lose the man she'd planned to spend the rest of her life with. What must it have been like for her to be widowed with a newborn? Claire didn't talk much about the family she'd left behind in California except to say that she didn't have a relationship with her mother—who'd left when Claire was seven—and that her father had his hands full with three kids from his second marriage.

"You know, it occurs to me that you haven't had any significant time off since you came to work for me,"

Linc said. "If you want to go visit your family over Christmas or Thanksgiving, I'm sure we could make that work."

Claire's eyes widened and she immediately started shaking her head. "That's really nice of you, but I remember how much you entertained last year, and now that you aren't seeing London, you'll be hosting all the parties."

"I don't have to be the host. My mother is always happy to show off the Mills-Forrest House."

"I wouldn't feel right about it," Claire said, smiling in a way that was both polite and firm. Arguing with her would get him nowhere.

"Fine, not the holidays, then. Maybe you could take some time off in January and go see them."

"I'll think about it."

"You know, Charleston is a great place to visit. You could invite them to come out here and see you."

She was shaking her head before he had even finished speaking. "With the kids in school and all their activities, it's just too hard for them to take time off during the winter. Plus, it's really expensive to fly everyone."

"What about your in-laws? How long has it been since they've seen their granddaughter?"

"Jasper didn't get along with his parents," Claire said in a breathless rush. "And didn't want them anywhere near his daughter. So it's really just Honey and me. She's all the family I need."

As close as Linc was to his mom and Sawyer, his father had been mostly absent during Linc's childhood, so he recognized Claire's reluctance to reach out. Had her family not been there for her after her husband's death? Was a lack of support the reason she came to Charleston in search of her ancestors?

Interesting about her great-great-grandfather's connection to Charleston. Linc didn't have a passion for the city's history like Sawyer and Knox, or his mother's obsession for improving the Thurston family's status in society, but he knew enough that the surname Robbins wasn't familiar. Likely, the entire story was little more than a family legend. Still, it wouldn't hurt to bring the matter to Sawyer's attention. Who knew what his sister might dig up?

As much as Linc wished they could linger over dessert and coffee, Honey was up past her bedtime and she was getting fussy. So he paid their bill and carried the sleepy toddler out to his car. As he buckled her into her safety seat, he considered what a contrast this evening had been to when he and London went out.

First of all, they'd rarely gone out alone. Even when they'd started the evening with a romantic dinner, inevitably the meal was merely a prelude for the main event, a gathering of friends at one of the local bars or the yacht club. Most of the time when they'd gone out, it was to attend a party or charity event. Sometimes it had seemed like the only time he and London were alone was when they were in bed.

While the low-key meal had given him an opportunity to get to know Claire better, he still sensed there was more to her that she didn't want to share. In the year since he'd hired her as his housekeeper, he'd held a picture of her in his head as sweet, earnest and haunted by her husband's death. Tonight's conversation had added dimensions to her personality and raised more questions than it had answered. She wasn't as uncomplicated as he'd thought.

"This was nice," Claire said as he eased the car out of the parking spot and headed for the exit. She sounded relaxed and a bit dreamy. "Thank you for dinner."

"I'm glad you enjoyed it." He had as well. So much, in fact, that he wanted to repeat it. "We should make a habit of it."

They were stopped, waiting for cars to pass so he could merge onto the main road. She turned her head so that she was no longer staring out the passenger window. Her eyes locked on him and he was besieged by the urge to slide his hand under her thick brown hair and draw her closer. Imagining the softness of her full lips yielding beneath a passionate kiss sent a flare of heat through his body.

"I'm sure you'd much rather be spending your time with your friends," she said and then yawned.

Despite his heightened awareness of the curve of her breasts barely outlined beneath the thin cotton of her sundress, he forced a light laugh. "Am I boring you?"

She covered her mouth and said, "Of course not. I'm just so full. I don't remember when I've eaten so much."

"It was a lot of food."

He tightened his hands on the wheel and told himself to relax. At an opening in the traffic, he sent the car surging forward. When the car was settled into the flow, he glanced at her and noticed her eyes were closed.

"As for spending time with my friends," he continued, "I get more than enough of their company. They like to go out, hit the bars and pick up women. It gets old. One thing I realized about myself after being with London is that I'm looking to settle down and have a family."

In fact, the escalating desire to become a dad had been one of the reasons he'd ended things with London. She'd been very clear that with her event-planning business starting to pick up, she didn't want to disrupt the momentum by starting a family.

"I think that will make your mother very happy," Claire said.

She was right, but he refrained from adding that he had to choose the right woman. And if his relationship with London had taught him anything, it was that making everyone happy was impossible. Dating London had made his mother miserable. His mother's not-so-subtle digs at London's "off" status had irritated him. Having the women in his life at odds was the furthest thing from peaceful. The question he had yet to settle was could he succeed in being happy if he married someone his mother was dead set against?

That was why this attraction he felt for Claire was eating him up. If he pursued her and desire turned to lasting love, there was no way his mother could ever accept that he married not just an outsider, but a penniless one as well. Claire lacked London's confidence and sophistication. Charleston society would eat her alive.

"What my mother doesn't realize is that I'm not interested in any of the women she might choose for me," Linc said.

"Don't underestimate her."

"Charleston has a limited number of old families, and I know nearly all of their eligible daughters."

"Don't forget you've been off the market for several years. Isn't it possible that someone new may have come on the scene? Someone who was previously unavailable?"

"I suppose." Although he wasn't feeling particularly hopeful. "But it's a long shot, don't you think?"

"With that attitude, you're probably right."

"Is that criticism I hear?"

"Of course not. I wouldn't presume…" she trailed off and stared at him with worried eyes.

"Relax. I'm not going to take offense," he told her. "I like to think you and I have become friends. And as such, I hope you feel comfortable telling me the truth."

"Sometimes I don't know how to be around you," she grumbled. "We laugh and get along so well, but in the end, I am your live-in housekeeper. You pay my salary and I don't want to step across a line."

"I'd never fire you because you said something I needed to hear. I'm not like that."

"Well, then, I guess I get to be more blunt." She shot him a wry smile, but her eyes remained cautious. "Just out of curiosity, what would it take for you to fire me?"

"If you were stealing from me."

"I'd never do that."

"Disloyalty." He noticed her confusion and elaborated. "Like if you decided to write a tell-all."

"I'm not sure there'd be any money in it. I think you're an open book. That's one of the things I admire the most about you. Despite the fact that you're a huge celebrity, you don't have any skeletons or dirty laundry in your closet. And I should know, since I clean your house." Her self-deprecating smile faded. "Since we're on the subject of public awareness, I should probably mention something that happened to me earlier today."

"What?"

"I met a woman at the grocery store who thought I was the reason you broke up with London."

Claire's declaration slammed into him like a fastball to the temple. At first, the words bounced around his stunned brain, but then he started to consider the implications.

"Do you know who she was?"

"Everly..." Claire shook her head. "I can't remember her last name, but she gave me her card." She reached into her purse and pulled out a small white business card. "Everly Briggs."

He tried to recall if he'd ever heard of her before. "Why would she say something like that?"

"I don't know." Scarlet swept up Claire's throat and flooded her cheeks. "She stopped me in the grocery store and we were talking about Honey, and then she noticed what I had in my cart and I accidentally told her I worked for you, and then she thought we were having an affair."

Claire ejected the explanation in a rush, not pausing for breath. As she stumbled to a halt, he glimpsed mortification and horror in her eyes, but guilt as well. Suddenly he felt a little light-headed. Because she was so devoted to Honey, he'd always perceived her as a devoted mom, first and foremost. Plus, she was still in love with her dead husband.

So where was the guilt coming from? Did she secretly desire him? The notion delighted him and awakened a whole new realm of possibilities.

"What did you say?" he asked, curious how she'd handled the conversation.

Her lashes flickered. "I told her that was ridiculous. That's not the sort of man you are, and there's nothing going on between us."

"Have you ever considered you're wrong about the kind of man I am?"

"Of course not." She looked startled. "You would never have cheated on London."

"You're right about that. Although, my reputation hasn't always been stellar. Knox, Austin and I used to tear up this town. Drinking. Hooking up with random women."

"But all that was before London. That's not who you are now."

Claire's fierce defense of him made his chest tighten. He doubted she'd rush to champion him if she knew how she'd featured in his dreams in the days and weeks before he'd ended his engagement. Her husband had been a hero. He'd died while serving his country. That man deserved Claire's love. The purity of her heart made Linc want to deserve her.

"Did she believe you?" he asked.

"Not at first, but then I set her straight."

Linc wished he'd been there to hear it. "How did you do that?"

"I explained to her that I clean your toilets and that's far from being romantic." Claire's dry tone didn't quite match the bright color in her cheeks.

"So you didn't clue her in to the skinny-dipping incident?"

"There was no skinny-dipping incident. Whenever I take Honey into your pool, I wear a very conservative one-piece suit." Her eyebrows drew together as she regarded him sternly. "This isn't funny. What if that's what everyone is thinking?"

"So what if it is?" Linc was completely intrigued by what Claire's body language had revealed. He offered her a lazy grin. If the gossip was widespread, they were already perceived as being guilty of having an affair. Part of him wanted to just go ahead and prove everybody right, "I'm sure everyone will congratulate me on my excellent taste in women."

She huffed impatiently. "You should be worried that it will appear as if you took advantage of someone you employ."

"Anyone who knows me will realize I would never do that. If anything happened between us, it would be because you couldn't keep your hands off me." His outrageous words produced a squawk of outrage.

"I am not seeing the humor in this," she said, her annoyance making her look more beautiful than ever.

Seeing that his teasing had taken her past her comfort zone, Linc sobered. "Are you worried about your reputation?"

"I'm your housekeeper. Why would I care what anyone thinks of me?"

"But you do," he guessed and could see from her expression that he was right. "Don't worry. No one who knows you would believe we were engaged in an affair, illicit or otherwise."

"Why is that?" she asked, her voice giving nothing away.

"Because everyone who knows you is aware..." He hesitated to continue, conscious of stepping over a line they hadn't to this point approached.

"Aware of what?"

"Your husband. That he was very important to you."

It occurred to him as he glanced her way, watching emotions play across her features, that he wanted her to deny how she continued to cling to her dead husband's memory. And why was that? As much as he wanted to, pursuing her was a bad idea.

"There are a lot of people who don't know me and will be quick to believe the worst," Claire said.

"Why do you care what those people believe? They are nobody to you."

"I don't. But you should. Those are your friends and neighbors. People in this town who matter."

"You don't think you matter? I do. You and Honey both."

"Well, of course Honey matters to me. And you matter to me. I mean, as my employer," she rushed on. "And your reputation matters to me. It should matter to you as well. Think of what your mother would say if she caught wind of the gossip. The whole thing could blow up into a huge scandal."

"You matter to me, too," he said, ignoring the latter

part of what she had said. When she gave a start, he wondered if his stronger feelings had leaked through. "You and Honey. And I don't give a damn about the gossip or what my mother thinks about it."

His phone began to ring and his sister's name flashed on the screen built into the car dashboard. As much as he wanted to ignore the interruption and continue this fascinating conversation with Claire, she'd wonder why he hadn't taken Sawyer's call.

"Hey," he said after keying in the call. "Claire and I are on our way back from dinner at a restaurant near Wappoo Creek."

After a brief pause, Sawyer asked, "You and Claire had dinner together?"

"It's our anniversary," he explained, wishing he didn't have to defend the act of taking Claire and Honey out for a simple meal. "She's been working for me for a year."

"Oh, sure. It's surprising how fast the time goes."

"You have that right. So, what's up?"

"We're finalizing the list of historic homes for our holiday tour and I want to make sure you're still willing to participate."

His sister was an active member of the Preservation Society of Charleston, working tirelessly to promote conservation of the city's historic homes and public buildings. In the fall, they offered several tours of historic homes and gardens. This year they were trying something new: a mid-December tour of homes decorated for Christmas.

"Do you have a date in mind?"

"It's probably going to be the second Saturday in December from two to five. We have six houses south of Broad participating at the moment."

"That should work out okay." Linc glanced at Claire. "Unless you can think of a conflict I've missed?"

Claire had been correct earlier when she'd mentioned how he liked to entertain around the holidays. He intended to host several events in December.

"That date should work," Claire said.

"Wonderful," Sawyer said. "Your house was so beautifully decorated for Christmas last year. I can't wait for people to see it."

When he'd purchased the Jonathan Elliot house several years earlier, the 1830s Greek Revival home from the antebellum period had been in rough shape, needing all new wiring and plumbing. Knox had spearheaded the project, coordinating the contractors, while Bettina had overseen the interior designer and given her opinion on all the finishes. The project had taken in excess of eighteen months and garnered him a Carolopolis Award from the Preservation Society of Charleston.

"You can thank Claire for the festive transformation," Linc said. "It was her vision."

"I'm sure she'll do just as wonderful a job this year," Sawyer said. "I have to run. See you tomorrow night."

"I'm looking forward to it."

Linc ended the call and shot Claire a glance. "No pressure," he said, amused by her scowl. "Just do what you did last year."

"Everyone will expect to be wowed again," she countered. "I have to come up with something even more spectacular."

"Whatever it is, I know it will be perfect."

"Why do you have such faith in me?" she demanded.

Linc shrugged. "You've never given me any reason to doubt you."

Something felt so right about donning her chef whites to prepare the dishes for Linc's dinner party. Claire was a little surprised how much she missed the hectic pace of a restaurant kitchen. Although she'd spent only a few years working alongside some really talented chefs in the San Francisco area, the experience she'd gained was immeasurable. And in moments like this, Claire wondered if she'd been a fool to give it up.

"Wow, it smells incredible in here." Linc's appreciative tones broke through Claire's musings.

Dressed in khaki pants and a pale blue button-down shirt with a white linen jacket and a bright blue pocket square that matched his eyes, Linc looked every inch the elegant Southern gentleman. During her time in Charleston, she'd noticed how the men of this town oozed charm and gracious manners that lulled a woman into thinking they weren't the least bit dangerous, while in fact they were heartbreakers one and all.

Claire doubted Linc had any idea just how devastating he could be to a woman's willpower through the simple act of sauntering into a room. His wavy blond hair was still damp and his elegant clothes couldn't camouflage the raw masculinity of his athletic body. She gulped in reaction to the sex appeal radiating from him.

"You smell pretty good yourself," she murmured, treating her nose to a deep pull of his scent as he came up beside her.

"Thanks, it's Armani's new cologne. They want me as their spokesmodel. My agent thinks I should do it."

"You'd be great." She had no trouble picturing his piercing blue eyes in magazine and television ads, inviting men and women alike to buy.

"I don't know. I've never considered myself a fashion guy."

"Well—" she cast her gaze over him and then zeroed in on his azure suede loafers "—you look pretty fashionable tonight."

He glanced down at himself. "You know my stylist does all my shopping. If it was left up to me, I'd be wearing jeans and a T-shirt."

And look amazingly hot in them. Honestly, the man could wear mud and look great. Sometimes just standing in the same room with all his gorgeous perfection made her ache.

"Is something wrong?"

Claire shook her head and turned her gaze away. "No." A flush crept up her cheeks and she hoped he would attribute it to the heat of the stove.

"Because the way you were staring at me just now…"

"Did you check the dining room to make sure everything looked okay?" It was a lame attempt to deflect his curiosity.

"I'm sure it's fine." Then he lowered his deep voice to a husky rumble that made her stomach drop and finished, "You look really professional in your chef whites."

"Thank you. I hope it's okay that I'm wearing them."

"Of course. You are a professional chef after all."

His nearness and the way his gaze lingered on the spot on her chest where her name was embroidered made Claire's heart bump like carriage wheels over cobblestones. Instinct warred with desire. Torn between stepping away and moving closer, her attention snagged on his lips and the tempting half smile that tugged one corner upward.

Handsome, powerful and forbidden. Any one of these qualities made him irresistible. Combined, they gave him an advantage that was entirely unfair.

"I noticed you're wearing your new earrings."

Linc touched the left one, sending it swinging. When it grazed the side of her neck, she shivered. There wasn't anything intimate in his manner, but her heart still raced with joy and longing.

"I really like them," she breathed, resisting the urge to rub at the goose bumps that had appeared on her arms.

"I'm glad." He dipped his head and peered more closely at the jewelry. "Yesterday, I wasn't sure if I'd chosen the right pair."

"I'm sorry if I seemed less than enthusiastic. I was a little overwhelmed by your generosity and the fact that you remembered my year anniversary." Not to mention there'd been that pesky longing to throw herself into his arms. "I can't believe how fast the time has gone."

"Claire."

Don't look at him. Don't look...

She might as well try to stop the sun from rising. His vivid blue eyes were mesmerizing. While it was true she'd shut down her sexuality, choosing instead to focus on being a mother, her body recognized the signs of sexual interest even as her brain denied it.

Linc, attracted to her?

Ridiculous.

Yet maybe not?

Living in such close proximity had enabled her and Linc to become friends of a sort. After all, Claire was the woman who took care of his house and fussed over him like a mother hen, making sure he ate well and providing a sounding board for him to share his thoughts. And in his vulnerable state after breaking off his engagement, he could feel safe around her because she was just his employee.

And that was all it should be between them.

Besides, she was wary of romantic entanglements after dealing with the way Jasper had changed over the course of their relationship. And Linc wouldn't repeat his mistake of falling for someone his mother didn't approve of. Claire put the brakes on her train of thought.

"I probably shouldn't say this..." He dragged his gaze over her lips.

Her dormant hormones flared to life. She swayed and placed her palm against the cool granite countertop to steady herself.

Falling for Linc was the height of stupidity, but how much harm could there be in tumbling into bed with him? Such an arrangement might benefit them both in the short-term. Besides, the gossip was already circulating about just such a thing. If she was already being blamed, why not actually be guilty.

"Say what?" she asked, losing her fight with temptation.

A knock sounded on the kitchen door. Regret filled her as she took a jerky half step away from Linc.

"That'll be tonight's waitstaff," she said in a breathless rush, "Your guests will be arriving shortly. You should…" Claire found herself unable to finish the statement. Her thoughts darted and spun, refusing to form any recognizable pattern. "Be ready to greet them," she concluded at last.

Linc's wide grin left little doubt he recognized his ability to fluster her. "I'll go do that."

Claire's knees wobbled as she made her way toward the kitchen door. She'd met the two people working for her tonight when she'd first arrived in Charleston. She and Jenny Moore had become friends and often met for lunch. Steve Henning was Jenny's boyfriend, and on a couple occasions, Claire had agreed to be fixed up with one of Steve's friends so the four of them could double date. While the evenings had been fun, none of the men had appealed to her enough to keep seeing them.

"Thanks for helping me out tonight," Claire said as she invited them into the kitchen.

"We're glad to be here," Jenny replied. She was a bubbly brunette who often spoke for the pair. "I can't believe we're serving for Linc Thurston's dinner party. Is he as gorgeous in person as on TV?"

"You'll have to see for yourself." Claire glanced at

Steve to see his reaction but glimpsed only fond amusement on his narrow face as he gazed at Jenny. They really were the cutest couple.

"Steve's nephew gave us Linc's rookie card," Jenny said, reaching into her purse and pulling out a card encased in plastic. "Do you think he'd sign it for him?"

"I'm sure he would." Claire glimpsed a bit of sparkle on Jenny's left hand and gasped. "You two are engaged? When did that happen?"

Jenny was glowing as she glanced up at Steve. "Last night."

"That's amazing." Claire wrapped her arms around her friend and squeezed, before turning to Steve. "I'm so happy for you both."

"We're pretty excited as well," Jenny said.

"Have you set a date?"

"We're thinking next April. Both of us have huge families, so the wedding is going to be big. We'll need lots of time to plan."

As much as Claire could've stood around and listened to Jenny describe her dream wedding, all three recognized they had a job to do. There would be plenty of time to talk after the meal was served and the guests left.

While Claire walked them through her menu and the wines she'd chosen, she noticed a trace of wistfulness threading through her emotions. Although she and Jasper had dated for several years, she'd never enjoyed the type of partnership Jenny and Steve had. Would she ever feel that with anyone? Should she settle for less? The thought didn't appeal to her. Yet she loved being a mom and wanted more children. And as much as she'd adapted to raising Honey on her own, she didn't want to slip up and get pregnant a second time without a solid commitment with the child's father.

The sound of the door chimes came from the front of the house. Linc's guests were starting to arrive. She needed to focus on the meal and push all unprofessional thoughts out of her mind. This proved easy once she heard all the laughter and jovial voices in the dining room. Claire was determined to make her first big dinner party for Linc memorable. She'd spent hours on the menu, deciding what flavor combinations might impress a group of people who were used to the finest.

"They're raving about your lamb," Jenny crowed as she entered the kitchen with an armload of empty plates. "I'd say Linc will be thanking you for making this dinner party memorable."

Claire smiled in pleasure as she assembled the final course. "I'm really glad. I was nervous that the food wouldn't be up to their regular standards."

"Are you kidding?" Jenny peered over Claire's shoulder as she plated the decadent chocolate cake with pomegranate sauce. "Your food rivals anything these types could find along King Street."

Her friend's praise warmed Claire. "Thanks."

As Jenny departed with the first of the desserts, Steve returned to the kitchen with another empty wine bottle and a message from Linc.

"He asked if you'd come in and meet everyone." When she hesitated, Steve handed her one of the desserts and motioned toward the dining room. "Come on. Take your bow."

Caving to Steve's encouraging smile and her own need to see Linc's reaction for herself, Claire carried in the final dessert plate and placed it in front of Linc. She then stepped back to survey the group.

The assembled guests were dressed for a formal dinner party with the men in suits and ties, while the women donned expensive cocktail dresses and jewelry. They sparkled and glittered beneath the dining room's large chandelier and Claire couldn't help but wonder which of them would be on Linc's arm at the next charity event or at the yacht club, helping him cheer on Knox during the upcoming regatta.

"This is Claire Robbins," Linc said with a smile. His eyes connected with hers, sending a light shiver down her spine. "You can thank her for the delicious dinner."

Claire had paired each course with a separate wine; most of the guests had the relaxed appearance of the mildly intoxicated. Still, she hoped that her food—and not just the wine—had contributed to the convivial atmosphere.

The redhead seated to Linc's right took note of Claire's chef whites. "Oh, you're a real chef. Where did you learn to cook like that?"

"I attended culinary school in San Francisco," she explained.

"And now you're Linc's housekeeper?" A blond man, his green eyes lazy as he sipped his wine, looked her over as if she was a piece of artwork he was evaluating. "Seems like your skills are wasted on him."

"Claire is a single mom," Linc jumped in before she could defend her choices. "Working for me is a lot less stressful than slaving away in a restaurant kitchen."

"Is that true, Claire?" A man with glasses and dark hair asked. "Is working for Linc as easy as he makes it sound?"

"He is gone over half the year." Claire masked her discomfort with a polite smile. "And I appreciate being able to spend so much time with my daughter."

"Honey is so sweet," Sawyer put in. "She just turned two a few weeks ago."

"I'll bet she's beautiful just like her mother," the blond man said.

"Actually, she takes after her father's side of the family," Claire responded with a polite smile. "Well, I'll leave you to your desserts. I'm glad you enjoyed the meal."

Returning to the kitchen, Claire regarded the dirty dishes piled on the countertops and sighed. She liked maintaining a neat, organized work space and this was far from it. Jenny was rinsing plates in the sink and piling them so they could be loaded into the dishwasher. Fortunately, all the china was dishwasher safe, so the only items Claire had to wash by hand were the antique crystal stemware.

"Thanks for getting this started," Claire said to Jenny.

"Are you kidding? You promised us leftovers. And I want you to know you can hire Steve and me to serve anytime. Linc Thurston is really nice. And most of his friends aren't too bad, either. You're really lucky to work for him."

"I am lucky."

Claire lifted her fingers to touch the earrings Linc had given her, remembering how his eyes had lit up earlier that evening when he noticed her wearing them. Just thinking about it sent her blood thundering through her veins. He'd almost looked…possessive. Which thrilled her even though she recognized the danger inherent in the feeling.

On the other hand, considering how well her food had gone over, perhaps he was a little concerned that one of his friends might try to poach her. The thought pleased her. Not that she'd ever consider leaving Linc. But it gave her ego a bump, thinking her skills might have garnered some interest.

While Steve kept an eye on things in the dining room, Jenny and Claire packed up the leftover food and chatted about Jenny's dream wedding. Claire could picture the low-country wedding on the grounds of an antebellum mansion. The ceremony would take place beneath oak trees dripping with moss, followed by an elegant reception beneath a tulle-draped tent.

"It's going to be beautiful," Claire said with a sigh. "Have you thought about colors yet?"

"I'm thinking a misty blue with accents of pale and bright pink."

"That sounds gorgeous."

"What colors did you have for your wedding?"

On the long trip from California, Claire had prepared for all sorts of questions about her wedding and marriage, so the lie came easily to her lips. "We eloped to Las Vegas and I carried a little bouquet of pink and white roses."

Jenny looked disappointed. "I couldn't imagine eloping. My family would be so disappointed. I'm the only girl, so my momma has been dreaming about my wedding for as long as I can remember."

"It wasn't like that for me," Claire said. "My mom left when I was seven."

And made limited attempts to stay in touch. This was what motivated Claire to devote her energy to Honey. She didn't want her daughter to know the slightest trace of neglect.

"I'm sorry," Jenny said, looking mortified. "I didn't realize that. You don't talk much about your family."

"There's not much to say, I don't speak with my mom and my dad has a wife and kids that keep him really busy." Hearing a trace of sadness in her tone, Claire forced a smile. "I have Honey, and she's all the family I need."

"But what about getting married again?"

"Maybe. I know it would be good for Honey to have a daddy, but I'm not sure I'm ready..." She trailed off and hoped Jenny wouldn't suggest another evening out with one of Steve's friends.

"I'm starting to get the picture."

Claire's gaze snapped to her friend. "What do you mean?"

"You have a thing for your boss. I don't blame you. He's hot. But don't let that get in the way of finding love."

"Linc?" Claire's voice broke a little as she said his name. "That's silly. Sure, he's charming and sweet, but he's way out of my league."

"He's out of nearly everyone's league. Unless you're a supermodel, sports star or a celebrity."

Jenny was right, and Claire considered how earlier she'd imagined Linc was attracted to her. What a ridiculous misconception that had been.

"Linc has nothing to do with my disinterest in hitting the dating scene," Claire said. "I'm just not ready."

"But you have a little crush on him."

Why deny it? "Well, of course. I'd have to be dead not to. But where he's concerned, I have my head on straight."

Five

The dinner party dissolved around ten o'clock with most of the guests departing for The Lucky Mojo, a rooftop bar featuring Cuban jazz music and salsa dancing. It was a favorite spot for their group of friends, who often ended the night there.

To Linc's surprise, Knox chose to stick around and join him poolside for a cigar and a glass of Glenmorangie Signet. Roses, hydrangea and freshly mowed grass scented the November evening. A cool breeze sifted through the crepe myrtle and palm fronds that provided shade for the private garden during the day.

"Nice party," Knox commented, nodding toward the lights still shining in the kitchen.

"Except for Austin and Roy," Linc countered. "Any

idea why they were acting like complete assholes tonight?"

"Roy has a thing for Della Jefferson." Knox enjoyed dishing on their friends and could be called on for all the latest drama. "But Austin got there first."

Austin had the money, looks and social position to have any woman in Charleston and used the triple threat to score as often as possible. Roy was an engineer from Savannah who'd gone to work with Boeing straight out of grad school. He liked to party and had been introduced to Austin, Knox and Linc after his attempt to pick up Sawyer at Burns Alley on King Street had met with devastating failure.

"Got to her as in slept with?" Linc rolled his eyes. "Didn't he know Roy took her out to dinner last week?"

"You know how Austin is. A different girl every night." Knox smirked. "He probably didn't even remember Della's name the next morning."

Linc considered that and wondered when Austin would stop acting like a frat boy. The guy was turning thirty. It was time to slow down.

"Do you think Roy is really into her?" Linc quizzed. "Or is he just pissed that Austin cut in on him again?"

Knox shrugged. "Between the two of them, Roy and Austin have slept their way through most of the eligible women in Charleston. I've never known either of them to get territorial before."

"Then maybe Roy does like her." Linc pondered the changes in their group dynamic as each of his friends began to settle down. "Speaking of people hooking up and/or dating, do you have any idea who Sawyer is seeing?"

Knox didn't miss a beat. "No. As far as I know, she isn't seeing anyone."

"That surprises me." Linc puffed on his cigar and stared at his friend. Had Knox's response been too carefully casual? "Usually you know everything that's going on with our circle."

"She hasn't said anything to me."

Linc considered this. Would Sawyer confide in Knox? She'd always viewed Linc's friends as a group of party boys, despite the fact that they all had successful careers. And she was right. Work hard and play hard. That was their motto.

"I thought maybe you'd heard something. You two cross paths all the time, know the same people. I can't imagine she could keep *everyone* from knowing."

Knox shook his head. "Have you asked her?"

"She told me to mind my own business."

"Shouldn't you do that?"

"I can't. She's seeing someone and doesn't want anybody to know. That piques my curiosity."

More than anything, Linc wanted Sawyer to be happy. It worried him that she was seeing someone and refused to come clean about the guy. What was wrong that she felt compelled to keep him a secret?

"Your sister is an intelligent, savvy woman. She doesn't need you playing interfering older brother."

"I didn't realize you were such a fan of my sister." Linc narrowed his eyes at his friend. "Are you seeing someone?"

"No."

"Have you ever considered dating Sawyer? You two have a lot in common, and I could think of worse brothers-in-law than you."

"Brother-in-law?" Knox looked shocked. "I'm not going to marry Sawyer. What is going on with you? Man, you need to get laid. Stop worrying about everyone else's love life and get one of your own."

Getting one of his own was what he was trying to avoid at the moment. Had he really almost kissed Claire earlier? The temptation to slide his fingers around the back of her neck and pull her close had almost overwhelmed him. The arrival of the waitstaff had happened about ten seconds too soon.

Linc shook free of the memory. "What's wrong with Sawyer?" he demanded, getting the topic back where he wanted it.

"Nothing. She's fantastic."

"But you wouldn't consider dating her?"

"I…" Knox trailed off, eyes wide as he contemplated Linc. "Why are you trying to fix me up with Sawyer?"

"I know you'd treat her well."

"What makes you assume that?"

"Because you know how protective I am of her and that would make you work damned hard to be sure she's the happiest woman on the planet."

"That is exactly why I'd never get involved with your sister. You are such a jerk to every guy she dates. No one is ever good enough. If she is seeing someone, it's no wonder she's keeping it a secret."

"I hate secrets," Linc said, thinking about how his

father's unwillingness to come clean about his bad business deals had caused him to sink deeper and deeper into trouble. "Nothing good comes of keeping the truth hidden no matter how bad it is."

"You should talk," Knox said, his tone loading the words with significance.

"What do you mean?"

"Your housekeeper?"

The sharpness of Knox's tone penetrated Linc's good mood. "What are you talking about?"

"Tonight at dinner. I saw the way you looked at her."

"How was that?" he asked lightly as if he didn't want to grab his best friend by his lapels and shake the answer out of him.

"Like you couldn't wait for the rest of us to get the hell out of your house so you could be alone with her."

"That's ridiculous." Linc made a scoffing sound to throw Knox off but saw that his friend wasn't to be deterred. "Claire works for me. That's all there is to it."

"And if she didn't?"

"She's still hung up on her dead husband."

"Are you so sure about that?"

"Yeah." Linc doubted his drawl gave anything away. "Why would you think otherwise?"

"Because there's the way she gobbles you up with her eyes."

Although Linc's heart stopped at Knox's observation, he'd spent enough time in the public eye to keep his expression under control.

"She doesn't." Linc frowned. *Did she?* The thought appealed to him. "You're making stuff up to mess with me."

"Only partially. I wanted to see your reaction."

"And?"

"You might not be sleeping with Claire, but you want to."

"And what's so wrong with that? She's beautiful, sweet, and we get along great." Wait…where was he going with this? Linc was supposed to be coming up with reasons why he didn't want to sleep with Claire.

"She's also your housekeeper," Knox pointed out unnecessarily.

"Men have been known to fall for their secretaries and nannies. Why not a housekeeper?"

Knox's eyebrows shot up. "Fall for?"

"Figure of speech," Linc said with a careless shrug. "Sounds better than 'sleep with.'" He rubbed his face. "Damn. I'm back in Charleston only a few weeks and my Southern manners kick in."

Knox laughed the way Linc had hoped he would, and for a few minutes, they smoked in companionable silence. It couldn't last. Linc could feel his friend's curiosity pressing on him even as he kept his gaze fixed on the tranquil turquoise pool glowing softly a few feet away.

"Why did you really break up with London?" Knox asked.

"I've already told you. Because I wasn't in love with her. And I don't really think she was in love with me."

"What makes you think that?"

Linc shrugged. "She liked the idea of what I represented, an old Charleston family. Ever since her family moved here, they've been trying to crack the 'inner circles' of Charleston society. London wanted to be a debutante and that was never going to happen. But if she married me and we had a daughter, she could live vicariously through her."

"You're not interested in all that stuff."

"I don't really care one way or the other."

"Are you sure about all this? She's been seen out with Harrison Crosby and he's the furthest thing from old Charleston as you can get."

"Trust me. London was obsessed with the whole society thing. So much so that every woman who attended tonight's dinner party has pulled me aside at some point since my engagement ended and given me an earful about my ex-fiancée."

Knox chuckled. "I'm surprised they waited that long."

"What do you mean?"

"A year ago, Augusta and Ruby approached Austin, Roy and me. They wanted us to warn you that London was too focused on your social position. I think they spent quite a bit of time chatting with your mother about it as well."

It wasn't a stretch to imagine how some of those conversations must've gone. Bettina often entertained his friends and saw nothing wrong with cultivating relationships with women she perceived as being more suitable for Linc to marry.

"Did London know that so many of my friends were rallying against her?"

"How could she not?"

That explained a lot of things. As his relationship with London had deepened toward marriage, she'd made it so that he spent less and less time with his old circle of friends. How ironic that the very people she wanted to associate with had shut her out and she'd responded by cutting them off from Linc. It had become a vicious cycle.

"I guess it's better for all of us that we're no longer getting married," Linc said.

"It's certainly better for your housekeeper."

Linc frowned at his friend. "Leave it alone."

"So you're not going after her?"

"No." He stared at the pool. "Maybe if things were different…"

If Claire wasn't still in love with her dead husband.

"You mean if she didn't work for you?" Knox asked.

"Yeah."

"You could always fire her."

Linc gave his friend a rueful grin. "I actually thought about it a couple days ago. But that would probably just make her hate me."

"What if she quit?"

"Why would she do that? She has a swell setup here, and I'm a great boss."

Knox finished off his scotch. "Ever think that Claire might be interested in turning in her French maid costume for a set of chef whites?"

Linc hadn't considered this. In fact, although he'd hired her more for her cooking skills than her cleaning abilities, there hadn't been much opportunity for him to utilize the former in the past year.

"She's happy right where she is."

"Maybe. But Austin was right when he pointed out that her culinary talent is wasted on just you."

"So I'll entertain more."

"Didn't you say she's catering your mother's party in a couple weeks?"

"Yeah. What of it?"

"Augusta cornered Claire just before we left and asked if she could do the food for the function she's coordinating next month for that free medical clinic her cousin volunteers at."

"Did she agree?" It hadn't occurred to Linc that Claire might be interested in picking up some extra work here and there.

"She said she'd think about it and give her a call."

Linc didn't consider himself selfish, but the thought of sharing Claire irritated him.

"Have you considered that you're doing her a disservice by having her as your housekeeper?"

"I guess I haven't."

Until now, he hadn't given it much thought. She seemed happy enough keeping his forty-five-hundred-square-feet home neat and clean. Often she pointed out that his long periods of absence during the spring and summer months enabled her to devote time and attention to her daughter. But now that Honey was getting older, wouldn't she be going off to preschool? Maybe with more free time Claire would start to explore opportunities where she could use her culinary skills.

And if Claire decided to quit and pursue a career as a chef? Linc fought down a rising uneasiness. The idea that his house would no longer ring with Honey's silver giggles or be filled with Claire's beautiful smiles made his gut knot.

"She won't leave me."

"What if she does?"

Something in Knox's tone snagged Linc's attention. He turned from his contemplation of the pool and noted his friend wore a concerned expression.

"She won't."

With Linc's guests gone, Honey finally succumbed to sleep. Although the rooms Claire and Honey occupied were on the third floor, noise from the boisterous dinner party had filtered up the stairs and the unusual activity in the house meant her curious daughter had resisted settling down for the night. Even though Claire had been the one to finally get Honey to fall asleep, she'd given the babysitter a little extra for her trouble.

Confident Honey was down for the night, Claire descended to the quiet kitchen to survey what still needed to be done. Since they'd finished most of the cleanup, she probably could've left the balance for the morning, but with euphoria pumping through her body on the heels of the successful dinner party, there was no way she was going to be able to sleep.

So, instead of pacing around her room or lying in bed and staring at the ceiling, Claire decided to wash the table linens and put away the crystal and china in the butler's pantry off the kitchen. With Honey's ever-increasing climbing ability, the sooner Claire could secure the breakable items, the better.

Claire padded barefoot into the kitchen. She'd exchanged her chef whites for what served as pajamas for her: a pair of blue-and-green-striped drawstring pants and a light camisole. Because it was cooler downstairs, she'd also slipped on a thin hoodie.

Under-cabinet lighting softened the stark white cabinetry and marble countertops, giving the kitchen a cozy feel. When Linc wasn't home, Claire often put Honey to bed and then came back to the first floor to fix a cup of herbal tea or enjoy a rare glass of wine. As much as she loved spending time with her daughter, Honey's high energy level left her needing a little peace and quiet at the end of the day.

She set the linen napkins to soaking in the laundry room and then carefully dried and placed all the china and glassware back where it belonged. Deciding she deserved a glass of wine after all her hard work, Claire chose one of the crystal goblets and poured some of the crisp leftover Soave that she'd paired with the scallops. A dry white from northern Italy, this particular vintage had notes of peach and marjoram. Savoring the flavor, Claire wandered into the dark sunroom and sat in her favorite chair overlooking the pool.

Several windows were opened to allow the cool night air to filter in. Cigar smoke drifted toward her on the breeze. Obviously, Linc hadn't gone to the bar with the rest of the party. And from the sound of things, he wasn't alone. Claire recognized the second voice as belonging to Knox Smith.

"Tonight at dinner," Knox said. "I saw the way you looked at her."

"How was that?" Linc asked, his tone light and unconcerned.

Claire knew she shouldn't stick around to overhear her employer's conversation, but curiosity kept her in place. Which of tonight's guests had piqued Linc's interest? From her brief glimpse of the assembled women, if she had to bet, Claire's money was on Landry, the stunning brunette with the green eyes.

It would be another adorable *L* and *L* combination. Linc and Landry. Like it had once been Linc and London. Plus, her rich sable hair would make for a nice contrast with Linc's blond all-American looks. The media would eat them up.

"Like you couldn't wait for the rest of us to get the hell out of your house so you could be alone with her," Knox replied, his tone dry.

"That's ridiculous." Linc sounded calm, almost bored. "Claire works for me. That's all there is to it."

They were talking about her. Shock and panic swamped Claire's lighthearted mood. She nervously rubbed her arms.

"And if she didn't?"

"She's still hung up on her dead husband."

"Are you so sure about that?"

"Yeah. Why would you think otherwise?"

"Because there's the way she gobbles you up with her eyes."

Claire shook her head, rejecting everything Knox was saying. It had been bad enough indulging her fantasy about sleeping with her boss, but that her interest in Linc was so obvious…

The heat of humiliation threatened to turn her to ash. What could be worse than having Linc's best friend point out her secret crush on him? She scooted forward on the chair, perched on the edge of the floral cushion. But instead of fleeing the room, she stayed to hear what Linc had to say about her in reply.

"She doesn't." Linc sounded doubtful. "You're making stuff up to mess with me."

"Only partially. I wanted to see your reaction."

And in turn, Claire wanted to pummel Knox. How dare he put ideas like that in Linc's head. The last thing she needed was for Linc to start questioning her reactions to him.

"And?"

"You might not be sleeping with Claire, but you want to."

Claire's thoughts flashed once again to the moment they'd shared before dinner. By the time she'd put the finishing touches on the dessert course, she'd convinced herself that she'd completely misread his signals.

"And what's so surprising about that?" Linc asked. "She's beautiful, sweet, and we get along great."

"She's also your housekeeper."

"Men have been known to fall for their secretaries and nannies. Why not a housekeeper?"

"Fall for?" Knox sounded surprised, but no more so than Claire.

Had she stepped into some sort of alternate universe where she had a shot with someone as wealthy and socially connected as Linc Thurston? Claire didn't know whether to laugh or cry.

"Figure of speech. Sounds better than 'sleep with.'"
A pause and then, "Damn. I'm back in Charleston only
a few weeks and my Southern manners kick in."

Jolted by the realization that she'd heard too much,
Claire got to her feet and moved like a ghost from the
room. Heart pounding, she stood in the kitchen, an
empty wine glass in her hand, her thoughts reeling.
She poured herself a second glass and sat at the breakfast bar to ponder what she'd overheard.

*You might not be sleeping with Claire, but you want
to.*

Was that true? It seemed impossible. Especially after
she'd glimpsed the beautiful, socially connected women
who'd come to his party. Surely he'd be more likely
to settle on one of them. Each one was sophisticated
and, if not wealthy, they sure dressed and shopped as
if the words *on sale* and *discounted* were not in their
vocabulary. They had grace and manners. Or if they
didn't, at least they'd been raised knowing how to behave in Charleston society. Claire thought back over
some of the conversations she'd heard Linc have with
his sister and Knox.

One thing about being a housekeeper, she was often
taken for granted. Like the furniture. People rarely
guarded their conversations around her, speaking of
anything and everything without fear of the information going anywhere. And why not? She was good at
keeping secrets. Her own and those of others.

Besides, what did she have to gain by taking gossip to the media? Nothing. Why risk her job? And Linc

had been good to her and Honey. She'd never do anything to harm him.

She's beautiful, sweet, and we get along great. What's not to like?

Like being the operative word. He liked her. She liked him. They'd become friends. To misinterpret something he said during a private conversation was foolish. Men talked about women and sex all the time. No need for her to go all stupid over it. She'd bet that every single one of Linc's friends had considered hitting on her at one point or another. Part of the reason she'd put on a wedding band and let everyone believe she was a widow was to avoid such awkwardness. If a man showed any interest in her, Claire merely whipped out her grief over her late husband and it shut down any advances.

Her status as a military widow had also lulled London's objections. Claire doubted that Linc would've been allowed to hire an attractive single mom as his live-in housekeeper, but a wife who was mourning the love of her life could be expected to keep her thoughts and hands off her employer.

When she heard the sound of a car door closing and an engine starting, Claire noticed the goblet was empty in her hand and was surprised how much time had passed. As the knob on the back door began to turn, she sat frozen at the breakfast bar, her cheeks heating as she realized she would have to face Linc after what he'd said about her. Why hadn't she gone upstairs?

"You're still up," Linc said, entering the kitchen.

"I came down to put everything away before morning." She gestured at the tidy, organized space with her glass. "And have some wine."

"You deserve to relax after such a long day."

"Just part of what I signed up for when I became your housekeeper." With her body moving of its own accord, leaning into the space between them, suddenly Claire recognized the importance of maintaining her distance. What better way than by bringing up her role in his house.

"Maybe, but you're more than just my housekeeper." *You might not be sleeping with Claire, but you want to.*

Heat flared as Knox's words came back to haunt her. "You did hire me for my cooking skills."

"They are pretty spectacular."

Claire sneaked several glances in his direction and decided the conversation she'd overheard earlier hadn't meant anything. Nothing about his expression gave any indication that he was attracted to her. Was she doing as good a job concealing her own feelings? Claire hoped so.

The last thing she needed was for Linc to pick up on her impossible longing for him. The best she could hope for was that he'd be flattered by her interest. The worst thing that could happen would be they'd cross a line, and then everything would blow up in her face. She couldn't risk having that happen. What if he kicked Honey and her out and she had to scramble to find a new place to live and work?

"You could've left everything until morning." His

gaze drifted from her eyes to her lips and then over her sleepwear. "Looks like you're ready for bed."

Claire cursed herself for trembling in reaction to his lazy smile. "I wouldn't be able to sleep, imagining the mess. You know how I am about the kitchen."

"Clutter is definitely your Achilles' heel." Linc set two crystal tumblers in the sink. "I challenge you to leave those unwashed until tomorrow."

"Ha ha. Very funny." But her fingers twitched as she regarded the dirty glasses.

"It's making you crazy, isn't it?"

"A little."

Bantering like this with Linc made it easier for her to ignore the drumbeat of her heart at his nearness. Did the man have any idea of the power of his sex appeal? How could he not with all the advertisers clamoring for him to represent their product, the Armani cologne being the latest?

He turned on the faucet and ran water into the glasses. "I'm happy to wash them. It's the least I can do after how hard you worked to make the dinner party a success." He gestured toward her empty crystal goblet. "If you're done with that, I can do it as well."

"I was just having a glass of wine," she replied, unsure why she felt compelled to explain herself. "Some of the leftover Soave."

"Which one was that?"

"The one I paired with the scallops."

Linc nodded. "That was nice. Dry with a note of peach." He arched an eyebrow at her. "What? You're surprised I remember it?"

"I did throw a lot of different wines at you."

"Showing off?"

"A little. I thought your first post-London dinner party should be memorable."

"You succeeded."

Claire immediately wished she hadn't mentioned London. "I'm sorry."

"For what?"

"I shouldn't have brought up London."

"I'm the one who ended the relationship," he reminded her. "The person who might be sensitive about discussing our breakup is London."

"I know, but you can't tell me that ending your engagement was easy on you."

"I feel guilty that I let it go on so long."

"You shouldn't. Sometimes falling out of love can sneak up on you in the same way falling in love does."

"What do you know about falling out of love?"

Although he didn't say Jasper's name, she suspected he was on Linc's mind.

"I'm not still hung up on my…" She couldn't call him her husband, couldn't speak the lie in this moment. "On Jasper." She delivered the statement with more heat than either of them had expected.

"Okay."

"You don't sound like you believe me." Now she was getting annoyed. "You know I've been out on several dates in the last year."

Linc's eyes widened at her fierceness. "Several dates," he mused. "Well, there you go. Sounds like you're ready to move on to the next stage in your life. Was there anyone special?"

His question flustered her. She opened her mouth to reply but had no idea what to say and set her hands on her hips in an imitation of Honey's terrible-twos willfulness.

"The point I'm trying to make is that I'm ready to move on. I just haven't found the right guy yet."

"You've always struck me as a woman who wants the right guy as opposed to a right-now guy."

"What does that mean?"

"That you aren't going to give someone a chance unless you can see yourself with him for the long-term."

"That just shows how little you understand me. Women have needs, too, you know. I have needs."

Linc nodded sagely, but the glint in his eye told Claire he wasn't done teasing her. "No doubt."

"I heard Knox teasing you about me." She cursed the husky note in her voice.

His expression turned to granite, all amusement gone. Looking chastened, he raked his fingers through his hair. "Damn, I'm sorry."

While her sensible side screamed at her to drop it, reckless urges had been building in her since he'd come home from Texas. The conversation she'd overheard combined with the two glasses of wine she'd consumed were making it hard to ignore her longing to press against the hard muscular body that was so close to hers.

"Don't be. It was my fault. I shouldn't have been eavesdropping. And it doesn't bother me that you've thought about sleeping with me." She got the words out only by studying the decorative marble backsplash behind the six-burner stove. This let her detach from the intensity of the exchange. "With our proximity…" She shrugged. "It only makes sense that you'd consider it."

He was silent for what felt like minutes, but based on the rapid thump of her heart, it was more like seconds.

"I think you're discounting how important you are to me. You and Honey." His fingertips grazed her knuckles. The fleeting touch awakened a kaleidoscope of butterflies in her stomach. "Have I thought about you in that way, sure. But you know I'd never take advantage of our situation in that way."

"What if you weren't taking advantage?" She couldn't believe such bold words spilled from her lips. What was she saying? He was her boss. "And it's not as if the gossip hasn't already condemned us."

"Claire." He sounded half amused and half despairing.

"Do you want to?" She shuffled forward until the heat of his body made her light hoodie unnecessary. Suddenly far too warm, she slid the zipper down and let it fall off her shoulders.

"Claire." This time when he said her name, there was a warning in it. He gripped her bare shoulders, sending shock waves of longing searing through her. "You have no idea what you do to me."

Linc's palms skimmed down her arms and gathered the cotton of her hoodie, pulling it up over her shoulders once more. She stood frozen as he covered her bare skin. Embarrassment spilled through her as she wondered what the hell had gotten into her.

"I'm sorry." Humiliated, she took a step back, surprised how hard it was to move away from him.

"No, I'm the one who should apologize. Knox and I should never have been talking about you."

"He's worried about you."

Despite Linc's rejection, her body continued to rumble with hungry impulses. While her brain screamed, *What were you thinking?* her body shouted, *Why did you stop?*

"I think he's more worried about you," Linc countered, his deep voice reverberating with regret.

"Why? You're his friend. If anyone stands to be hurt, it's you."

Linc cocked his head. "How do you figure?"

"Your reputation."

"To hell with my reputation. That's important to my mother, not to me."

"But your mother is important to you. Imagine how something like you being discovered sleeping with your housekeeper would hinder her mission to find you a suitable Charlestonian woman to marry."

Linc expelled his breath on a derisive snort. "My mother has weathered bigger scandals just fine. Besides, what she wants for me is not necessarily what I want for myself."

"You mean you don't want to marry a girl from a good family and start having children?"

"I want to marry a woman I love. I don't care what sort of a family she comes from."

While his determination was sexy and thrilling,

Claire knew that his engagement to London had strained his relationship with Bettina.

"That's all well and good," she said, "but your mother does care, and in the end, you know that matters to you."

And there was no way Bettina Thurston was going to approve of her son getting into any sort of relationship with his housekeeper.

Six

Claire's words infuriated him because he knew she was right. But he didn't want it to matter that his choice of a fiancée had upset his mother when he and London were engaged.

"I like to think she'd eventually come around if she knew it would make me happy."

"Your mother is a strong matriarch who believes she knows what's best for you."

Linc couldn't argue with that. She'd certainly recognized that London wasn't the girl for him. He eyed Claire. No doubt his mother would have an even stronger aversion to his starting up with his housekeeper. He raked his fingers through his hair, utterly at war with himself over what he wanted and what he knew to be the best thing to do.

Before Linc could fall victim to his conscience, he reached out and curved his fingers around the back of Claire's neck. Her hand came up between them, the side of her fist resting lightly against his chest. He expected her to push him away and was surprised when her fingers wrapped around his lapel and tugged him toward her.

Dipping his head, he grazed his lips over hers, noting her soft murmur of pleasure. For a second, she leaned into him, her slight weight a sensual blow that knocked his thoughts askew. His heart pumped like he'd run a mile full-out.

"Claire." He went back for a second taste, lingering over her soft lips.

But before he could kiss her yet again, she set her fingertips against her mouth and ducked her head.

"I've been dying to do that since last night," he admitted, setting her free and taking a step back. His hands shook, so he shoved them into his pockets. What was this strange power she had over him that a single chaste kiss turned him inside out?

"I thought it was just me."

Thoughts flitted through his head, none lingering for more than a second.

Mistake. Again. She wants this. I want this. No. Yes.

But what it came down to, what kept him from reaching for her a second time, was the consequences for both of them. She had Honey to think about. He didn't want to jeopardize her future if he pushed forward with this attraction between them.

He needed to know if he was just reacting to something forbidden, or if she was as desirable as he imagined. In truth, he wasn't sure if he could answer any of these questions. In his younger days, he'd never had to pursue women. They had just fallen into his lap like overripe fruit. Nor had London given him a run for his money. Things between them had been easy and familiar right off the bat. In fact, he couldn't think of a single woman he'd ever chased. He was too busy putting all his energy into baseball.

"I'd better get the china and crystal put away," Claire said as she rinsed out her wine glass and set it in the sink.

"My offer to help still stands."

"Thanks, but it won't take me very long."

In a strange way, he felt dismissed. Clearly, she was trying to reestablish the nature of their relationship. Employer and housekeeper.

Instead of arguing, Linc headed upstairs to the large master bedroom on the second floor. As he trudged up the wide staircase, he stripped out of his blazer and unbuttoned his shirtsleeves. He'd scarcely entered his bedroom when his ears picked up the soft squeak of a pine board in the hallway behind him. Tossing his coat onto a nearby chair, he turned and spied Claire standing just outside his room.

"I'm sorry about what happened earlier," she said, uttering the last thing he wanted to hear. "I've put you in a bad position."

"You haven't." He watched as she covered one bare foot with the other and seemed to withdraw into herself as if trying to disappear.

She cleared her throat. "Can we chock it up to…"

"Moonlight?"

Her lips twitched in a familiar wry smile. "I was going to say curiosity."

"But that's not all it was." He stepped into the hallway, body coming alive as he drew within arm's length of her.

"I didn't realize until recently just how much I ignored my own needs."

"You've had Honey to think about."

He wasn't going to bring up her devotion to her deceased husband again. Obviously, she was ready to move on. Or she thought she was.

"She's been my priority, but I also think I've used her to isolate myself. The only way I've ever successfully conquered loneliness is to keep busy and stay focused."

"I'm familiar with the technique. How do you think I got so good at baseball? During the years that my father was in prison, I spent hours and hours at the batting cages or running catch-and-throw drills."

"I get that."

Linc reached out and set his fingers beneath her chin, tipping her head back so he could drown in her big brown eyes. "I'm here for you. Whenever you need me."

"Some uncomplicated sex?" Her tone was light and teasing, but her somber expression betrayed her nervousness.

"Whatever you need." He shaped his grin so she could either take his offer seriously or dismiss it as a joke. He hoped she chose the former.

She sighed. "You have no idea how much I want to take you up on that."

"Hopefully as much as I want you to."

"Oh, hell."

And then she was taking him by the hand and drawing him back into his bedroom. It was the sign he'd been waiting for. With a relieved sigh, Linc strode forward, scooped Claire into his arms and carried her purposefully toward his bed.

He set her down on the coverlet and stripped off his shirt. Eyes never leaving her, he made quick work of his shoes and watch. While he was thus occupied, she peeled her hoodie off and tossed all the decorative pillows aside.

"I make your bed every morning and never found all these things to be as annoying as I do right now." Her unsteady breath and wicked grin had a predictable effect on his arousal.

"Will it shock you to know how many times I've wanted to surprise you in the act of making the bed and tumble you into the sheets?"

"Would it shock you to know how many times I've pressed my face into your pillow and imagined what it would be like to be naked in this bed with you?"

He groaned. "You win."

"Tonight, I think we both win."

He unfastened his belt buckle and popped open the button on his pants, but when he noticed she was lifting her top over her head, he stopped to watch. Inch by gorgeous inch, her naked torso came into view. He stopped breathing as the pale blue fabric rode up over the lower curve of her breasts. And then suddenly her dusky nipples appeared and his mouth went dry.

As soon as she'd stripped the shirt off, he encircled her tiny waist with his hands and drew her toward him. She hummed joyously as his mouth came down over hers. Her fingers skimmed over his shoulders and sank into his hair, tugging fiercely as her lips parted beneath his to allow the thrust of his tongue.

Her hardened nipples raked his chest, her passion driving his desire even higher. He stroked his palms up her back, feeling her muscles shift beneath her silky skin. Leaving one hand to delve into the satin curtain of her hair, he sent his other down her spine to the small of her back. She shivered and moaned as he delicately caressed the indents on either side of her spine, before sliding his hand beneath the waistband of her pajama bottoms and cupping her bare butt.

"Linc." His name broke from her lips as he kissed his way down her neck to the sensitive hollow of her throat. "That feels incredible."

"I haven't begun to make you feel incredible yet," he replied, determined to rein in his lust so he could make this a night she'd never forget.

"Pretty much everything you do is wonderful."

"It feels like you set the bar too low."

"I don't want to put any pressure on you."

Her lopsided smile set him on fire, but it was the sudden flash of shyness he glimpsed that enabled him to calm down.

"How long has it been for you?" he asked, wanting to take things slow and make it perfect for her. She deserved to be cherished and that was what he intended to do.

She bit her lip and thought about it. "Since the night Honey was conceived?"

Wondering if that was guilt flickering in her eyes, Linc did the math. Almost three years. Damn. The knowledge that he would be the first man to have her since her husband cooled his ardor somewhat. Instinctively, he knew he wasn't competing with the man, but how could she help but compare them?

Her palms framed his face, bringing him back to the moment. "Tonight, there's only you and me."

It didn't surprise Linc that she had a knack for reading his mind. From the beginning, she'd anticipated his needs. Sometimes it was disturbing, but mostly he enjoyed the hell out of it. Once, he'd seen a three-foot-tall tiger displayed in a toy store window and pictured her buying it for Honey, just to see if he and Claire were communicating telepathically. And two weeks later, she'd bought her daughter a stuffed cat. Granted, it wasn't the three-foot-tall tiger, but she definitely picked up on the vibe he'd been sending.

"I'm glad to hear that. I've never had a threesome."

She paused in the act of sliding her fingers along his abdomen and hit him with a dry look. "Never?"

Despite her doubting tone, Linc spied hope in her expression and promised never to do anything that would erase her faith in him.

"You say that as if you think I'm some sort of player."

"Not a player," she corrected. "But you are a sports

star. Women must throw themselves at you all the time. I imagine you've had plenty of opportunities."

"Oh, I've been approached, but I like my women one at a time. It gives me an opportunity to focus all my attention on what gives them the most pleasure." He gave her butt a little squeeze and heard her light gasp. "You'll find I like to be very thorough."

She ran her finger down his fly. "No more of that until I get your pants off."

"Let me take care of that for you." He brushed her fingers aside and slid his zipper down.

As much as he'd enjoyed the glancing contact of her hands on his erection through two layers of clothing, more than anything he wanted to feel her skin sliding along his hardened length. But it was much too early for that. He slipped off his pants but kept on his boxer briefs.

"Three years is a long time," he murmured, sliding his fingertips beneath the waistband of her pajama bottoms and carefully easing them down her hips. "I'm going to take things slowly. We have no need to rush."

As the cool air touched more of her skin, Claire gasped and her trembling increased. Linc coaxed her onto her back and skimmed her cotton pants off her legs. He drank his fill of her naked body, gaze skimming over her small breasts and flat stomach. The indent of her waist and her long, slender legs. How had he not realized how beautifully put together she was?

"Is everything okay?" she asked, her voice sounding rusty from disuse.

"Just about perfect," he replied, settling onto the bed

and moving between her thighs. "I want to kiss every inch of you, but right now I need to start here."

"Are...are you sure?" she stammered as he leaned forward and gave her one long lick. "Oh, yes," she moaned, answering her own question.

He went back for a second taste, liking the way her flavor filled his mouth and her sexy groans caressed his ears. She wasn't quiet, and her unsteady exclamations of pleasure drove him on. It didn't take him long to figure out exactly what she liked. He debated urging her into a fast orgasm or letting one build until she was out of her mind.

In the end, what decided him was the three years she'd gone without making love. As much as he wanted this moment embedded in her psyche forever, he knew how he'd feel if he'd been celibate that long. As it was, Claire was the first woman he'd slept with since ending his relationship with London. While all his friends had encouraged him to jump straight into the dating pond again, the reason why he'd broken off his engagement was the woman currently occupying his bed. He couldn't deny it any longer. Why settle for hamburger when what he craved was a Japanese Wagyu striploin.

Claire came for him with a startled cry as if she hadn't expected to climax. The sound stripped his soul bare, so he kept going, digging his fingertips into her hips to keep her tight against his mouth as he drove her harder.

"No. No. It's too much." Her body shuddered and quaked as she continued to orgasm. "Linc, I can't..."

But she could. And she did. Beautifully.

As she lay gasping for breath, he kissed his way back up her body and gathered her into his arms, ignoring the sharp bite of lust so he could soothe her with gentle kisses and soft murmurs. His emotions tangled as she murmured his name.

"Don't thank me yet," he replied. "We've only just gotten started."

She threaded her fingers through his hair and seized his lower lip between her teeth, growling playfully at him. "You're such an amazing man—"

He didn't want her praise, didn't want to think about her comparing him to the husband she'd lost. Instead, he kissed her deeply, until there was nothing but her heat and the softness of her skin beneath his hands and his lips.

"I have to have you," he murmured, his tongue swirling around her nipple.

"I'm all yours."

The steamy rasp of her voice only added to his excitement and Linc knew if he didn't get a condom rolled on in the next few minutes, there was going to be trouble. She watched him from beneath her lashes through the entire procedure, but when he shifted between her spread thighs and positioned himself at her entrance, he saw that her eyes had drifted closed.

"Open your eyes," he commanded. "I need to know you're with me."

She smiled languidly, lifting her hips so that he slipped a little ways inside her. "I'm here."

And when she did as he requested and met his gaze with her own, he plunged inside her in one smooth stroke. She whimpered and arched her back, accepting every inch of him. Gliding into her wetness proved to be mind-altering. Her long celibacy made her so tight that by the time he was seated deep in her heat, he was reeling.

Grinding his teeth together to keep himself from coming, he glanced down and saw her lips curve into the most glorious smile he'd ever seen. With his brain waging a fierce battle against his body, Linc began a steady, torturously slow rhythm, determined to give her everything he had and more.

"You are so tight," he groaned. "You're driving me crazy, Claire."

In answer, her snug, slick walls pulsed around him and he began pumping into her harder, going as deep as he could. She met each thrust with a little chant and sank her nails into his skin.

"More," she begged. "I want all of you."

So he gave her everything he had. His breath rasped against her neck as he filled her again and again. Reaching between their bodies, he cupped her, putting the perfect pressure on her clit.

"Come for me."

And then she was. With a long, searing cry, her body began to shake. Linc clamped his mouth over hers, drinking her pleasure as her body gripped him and started a chain reaction that sent him soaring off a cliff right after her.

Ten days before Bettina's party, Claire took her culinary expertise to the Mills-Forrest House and spent several hours preparing a selection for Linc's mom to choose from. Although Bettina had a reputation for being a tough cookie, Claire had always gotten along well with the Charleston matriarch.

And Claire wanted to keep it that way, which was why for the past couple days her focus had been on brainstorming dishes and assembling her menu. Not on daydreaming about the magical night she'd spent with Linc.

Today's plan was for her to serve her menu ideas to Bettina as a mid-afternoon snack. While she was occupied doing this, Linc had offered to take Honey to the Children's Museum of the Lowcountry so she wouldn't have to hire a babysitter.

It still perplexed her that he enjoyed spending time with the two-year-old. Honey could be challenging at times, although the toddler's sunny personality made up for the worst of it. But Linc was fond of Honey and, of course, she adored him. Watching them together made Claire's heart ache because it reminded her that Honey would never know her father. And despite how Jasper had begun changing as his many tours overseas took their toll on his psyche, from the expression on his face when he held Honey in his arms at the hospital, Claire knew he would've done anything for his little girl.

Dolly was ironing sheets in a small nook near the kitchen when Claire carried in several grocery bags of ingredients. The older woman scowled as she watched Claire unpack and arrange things on the enormous marble island.

"I told her I'm not helping with the cooking for the

party," Dolly said with an imperious sniff she'd picked up from her longtime employer.

"You already do so much for Bettina," Claire said, her tone soothing. "I wouldn't want you to feel pressure to do more. So I hired waitstaff and an assistant to help me prepare all the food."

With a satisfied nod, Dolly returned to her task, and for the next two hours, the two women worked in companionable silence. For her part, Claire was happy to not have to chat.

As she was finishing up, she heard the distant sound of the doorbell ringing. Fortunately, Bettina had warned her that she was inviting some of her friends, so Claire had come prepared with enough food. While Dolly headed off to welcome the guests, Claire put the final touches on her plates, wondering whom she might encounter today.

Promptly at four o'clock, she carried the first two offerings out to the dining room and found five women sitting around the table. Besides Bettina, Sawyer and her friend Augusta, who'd approached Claire after Linc's dinner party about catering the food for a fundraiser, there were two women in their early forties.

"Good afternoon, ladies," Claire said, setting her first menu items on the table. "Today, I have for you a mozzarella and grape tomato skewer with basil drizzled with a balsamic reduction, as well as a salmon and cream cheese bite."

While Dolly set about pouring glasses of white wine, Claire went back into the kitchen to fetch serving plates with spicy tuna wrapped in pickled cucumber, baked brie with walnuts and pistachios, and yellow tomato gazpacho shooters with basil crab salad crostini.

One of the first chefs Claire had worked for had been a stickler for presentation and had hammered into his employees that food needed to be visually pleasing as well as a festival of flavors. That was why she'd made certain that each selection she presented to Bettina was not only a treat for the palate, but interesting to the eye as well.

By the time she finished setting the last of her eight plates on the table, the women were exclaiming over the food. A warm sense of accomplishment flooded Claire. Cooking was her passion and it thrilled her when people enjoyed what she lovingly created.

"In addition to these," she said, making eye contact with Sawyer, who gave her an encouraging smile, "I thought we should have boiled shrimp and a cheese platter. And I have a friend who is an excellent pastry cook. For dessert, I could order up a selection."

"This is all quite nice," Bettina said, proving far less difficult to please than Claire had anticipated. "I approve of everything."

"Wonderful."

"I agree," Augusta spoke up. "This is all amazing."

Buoyed by all the positive feedback, Claire grinned. "I'm glad you like it."

Augusta indicated the two woman who'd accompanied her. "Let me introduce you to these ladies. This is Genevieve Brand and Portia Hillcrest. I brought them along today because they are in charge of organizing the charity polo match to support the local YMCA next

Saturday, and they were hoping you could help them out of a jam."

Genevieve Brand was nodding as Augusta spoke. A thin woman with sleek blond hair and a smooth round face, Genevieve wore a beautiful pale pink suit and a triple-strand pearl necklace that looked like it cost more than Claire had paid for her Saab.

"Our caterer had a family emergency and canceled last minute," Genevieve said. "We are in a terrible predicament with the event coming up so soon and no food. Would you be able to help us out?"

Claire's first impulse was to say no. When Augusta had approached her after Linc's dinner party, asking if she would be interested in catering an event in the future, Claire hadn't dreamed anything would come up so soon. She didn't have the facilities or the staff to handle a large party.

"I'd have to talk to Linc." When Genevieve and Portia exchanged a confused look, Claire explained, "I'm his housekeeper."

"I'm sure he'll say yes." Augusta beamed as if everything was settled. "It's one of his favorite events, after all."

"Does he play polo?" The question slipped out of Claire's mouth before she could stop it.

Sawyer laughed. "No, but he's big on any charity that helps out kids, and he loves rooting for Austin."

"By rooting for," Bettina murmured wryly, "Sawyer means betting on."

"There's always a little friendly wagering that goes

on during the match," Portia explained. "Those proceeds also go to the charity."

"Sounds like a worthwhile event," Claire said, a little overwhelmed by the weight of these women's expectations. "Still, I should run it by Linc."

"Of course."

"Run what by Linc?" came the question from the doorway.

Claire's eyes snapped to her employer and her heart skipped a beat. Nor was she the only one affected. A collective sigh went up from the room's occupants as each took in the charming picture of the gorgeous blond man with an armful of adorable toddler. It was hard for Claire to keep her expression neutral as she was suddenly besieged by the memories of his touch.

"Genevieve and Portia need Claire's help with the charity polo match next Saturday," Augusta said to him. "They lost their caterer at the last minute."

"What an adorable little girl," Portia exclaimed, looking perplexed.

"This is Honey," Linc said, his smiling blue eyes landing on Claire.

"She's Claire's daughter," Bettina clarified, her tone flat.

"How was the children's museum?" Claire asked. "Did she behave herself?"

"She was a perfect angel."

"I don't believe you," she replied, all too aware that their exchange was being closely observed.

"You know she always behaves for me," Linc said, shifting his attention to Honey. "Don't you?"

"Yes." The little girl patted his cheek with her palm and giggled.

"They had a fire truck exhibit. She was a huge fan."

"Whoooo, whooo." Honey sounded more like an alarm than a train.

"It was nice of you to take your housekeeper's daughter to the children's museum," Genevieve murmured, mild judgment in her tone.

When Claire stiffened at the remark, Linc shot the woman an uncompromising look.

"She's catering my mother's party as a favor. The least I could do was save her from having to hire a babysitter today."

While everyone nodded, Claire stood frozen with humiliation. Once again, it was pretty obvious in the eyes of many people that a clearly defined line existed between the haves and those who work for them.

"Why don't I take Honey now," Claire said, sliding around the outer perimeter of the room in Linc's direction. "You should sit down and visit with these ladies. I can bring you a plate if you'd like to taste the food."

"No, thanks. Honey and I are going to hang out in the kitchen with you while you finish up."

Curiosity was almost palpable in the dining room.

"Before you go, Linc," Genevieve said. "Can you give Claire permission to work our fund-raiser? She won't do it without your approval."

Linc shook his head. "She doesn't need my permission. She's free to do whatever she wants with her weekends."

All eyes turned in Claire's direction as he finished

speaking, and she felt like a rabbit that had stumbled into a wolves' den.

"Then I guess my answer is yes," she said, eager to escape a situation that had suddenly become awkward and embarrassing. More than anything, she wished the scene with Linc and Honey hadn't played out in front of these women. Gossip around town already had it that there was something going on between her and Linc. Thanks to his arrival, it was pretty obvious that Claire and her employer were friends and possibly a little too comfortable with each other.

As she left, her gaze fell on Bettina. Linc's mother wore a slight frown. Claire returned to the kitchen, hoping Bettina wasn't concerned that Linc had babysat Honey.

"Thank you for watching Honey for me today so I could concentrate on getting everything ready," she said. "If you want to leave her with me and head out…"

"I don't have anything else to do this afternoon, so I'm happy to hang out with her until you're done here," Linc said, setting Honey on the ground and finding her a couple pots and a wooden spoon. He then demonstrated drumming on the cookware and the toddler set to work making noise.

"Thanks," Claire mumbled, rinsing the last of the plates and loading them into the dishwasher.

While she finished up, Linc leaned on the counter and surveyed the leftovers. "How did the tasting go?" He reached out and snagged one of the appetizers, popping it into his mouth. "This is fantastic. What is it?"

"Puffed pastry with caviar." Claire dodged around

Linc and began packing up the leftovers. "Your mom liked everything."

"Terrific." He tried a tartlet with goat cheese and fig and moaned appreciatively. "Then why are you upset?"

"I'm not upset."

"Is it because they badgered you into catering the charity polo match next week?" He grinned at her over a shot glass of gazpacho. "Don't do it if you think it's going to be too much."

"It isn't that…" She trailed off, not wanting to get into her concerns right there in his mother's kitchen.

"Is it the reason my mother is having the party?" He lowered his voice until only she could hear him. "Are you worried that I'm going to meet someone? Because if that's it, you don't need to give it a second thought. I'm only going through the motions to satisfy my mother."

Claire stopped what she was doing and gave him her full attention. Was she acting like she was jealous? They'd slept together only once and she hoped she'd been clear about it not becoming a habit.

Yet, if she investigated her churning emotions, she suspected the fear in her heart had little to do with concern over whether his next serious relationship would want the live-in housekeeper fired. Claire suspected she was well on her way to falling for her handsome, charming employer.

"You need to take her matchmaking more seriously," Claire said, denying the truth staring her straight in the face. "She has only your best interest at heart."

"That doesn't sound like the sort of advice I'd expect from a woman who had her world rocked by me a few nights ago."

"My world rocked?" Claire repeated in a barely audible whisper while glancing toward the hall that led into the dining room. Embarrassment and desire warred inside her. "Can we not talk about this here?"

"Relax." His voice was a husky rasp across her senses. "No one can hear us."

"Nevertheless." She tried for crisp and professional but came across tremulous and disturbed. Her breath hitched as his fingers tugged at her chef jacket, making the fabric slide across her overly sensitive skin. "Linc."

"You know it's going to happen again. Tonight, I think." His eyes glittered, making it impossible for her to look away.

"I don't know that." But she wanted it to. So badly. Her entire body screamed for him to kiss her. Caution was quickly drowning beneath the flood of desire. "Linc," she almost pleaded. "It was supposed to be one and done. Just two people who turn to each other in a moment of weakness."

She managed to tear her gaze away and shot a glance toward the dining room. To her relief, no one was skulking in the butler's pantry, listening to them, but she really didn't want to talk about this anymore.

"Weakness?" He took his time tasting the word. "Yeah, I guess that sounds about right. When it comes to you, my willpower is shot to hell."

"Linc, please." She was begging now through clenched teeth.

"Those were your exact words that night."

"Oh, Linc…"

The heat scorching her cheeks wasn't caused by the temperature in the kitchen. She hungered to take hold of Linc's knit shirt and drag it over his head. To feel his hands slide beneath her chef whites and claim her breasts.

He set his palm on the kitchen island and leaned toward her, pitching his voice to a sexy murmur that made her muscles bunch in anticipation.

"'Oh, Linc…' I'm going to make you say them again," he vowed, his whole manner leaving no doubt that he wouldn't stop until she'd given him everything he wanted. "And again."

Pledge delivered, he stepped back, leaving her quaking and achy and oh, so ready to do anything he asked. From the satisfaction glinting in his eyes, he knew what his words had done to her. A second later, he scooped Honey into his arms and carried her out the kitchen door, and Claire watched after him, a trembling bundle of unsatisfied longing.

Seven

The opportunity to lure Claire back into his bed failed to materialize in the days that followed the tasting at his mother's house. Claire was completely engrossed in preparations for the party, and while he missed spending time with her, Linc appreciated her passion and wanted her to shine. At least that was what he told himself as his ache for her grew.

At eleven o'clock on a Saturday—far too early for him to be coming home from a night out with the guys—Linc eased his BMW into the driveway and parked beside Claire's ancient Saab. He shut off the engine and in the ensuing silence listened to the insects drone. His jaw ached from grinding his teeth. The whole evening had tested his patience as he watched his friends hit on a variety of women and compete to see who could take the prettiest one home.

Usually he found their antics amusing, but ever since he'd warned Claire he intended to make her moan for him again, he'd been distracted and edgy.

In fact, he hadn't planned to go out at all tonight. He'd intended to stay close to Claire in case she wanted to knock off early and hang out, but she had plans of her own. Since he hadn't been all that keen on staying home alone, he'd let Knox and Austin drag him out. He'd pretty quickly discovered that being by himself wasn't the problem—it was being away from Claire. She'd become like a drug in his system. No one but her appealed to him.

It hadn't helped that he'd caught a glimpse of London having dinner with Harrison Crosby as he headed toward The Lucky Mojo. She'd looked as elegant and unflappable as ever, but something about the way her date smiled at her kicked Linc in the gut. He recognized a man on the hunt. He'd seen the same expression reflected in his mirror over the past several days.

While he didn't begrudge London her happiness, Linc couldn't help but experience a small flash of envy that Harrison could wine and dine her to his heart's content, while Linc was left skulking around in secret with Claire.

Linc didn't give a damn who knew he was pursuing her, but Claire was sensitive about the situation and worried because she worked for him. Although he didn't want to add to her concern, Linc sensed that by keeping their budding relationship quiet and acting like being with her was something he was ashamed of, she would never believe their divergent social positions didn't matter.

As he stepped out of the BMW, the sound of splashing came from the direction of the pool. He headed for the source of the noise. The thick vegetation surrounding the concrete pool deck gave him cover as he lurked and watched Claire make her way from one end of the narrow pool to the other with slow, lazy strokes.

Tonight, she wore a utilitarian black one-piece that did nothing to enhance her slender curves. Even so, Linc found himself mesmerized by the flash of her slender arms and legs as she negotiated a flip turn and resumed her smooth rhythm. She was swimming for pleasure rather than fitness, but there was no missing the precision in her strokes. She moved like a trained swimmer and this showcased yet another example of how little he knew about her.

When she drew close to the end nearest him, Linc stepped out of the shadows and approached the turquoise water. "It's a little chilly for a night swim, isn't it?" He figured the air temperature was around sixty.

"You keep the pool at a comfortable eighty-two degrees, so it doesn't bother me until I get out." She frog kicked to the edge and looped her arms over the concrete.

The dark smudge of mascara beneath her eyes gave her an edgy look he appreciated. He imagined licking the water from her throat as her legs wrapped around his waist in the weightless environment.

"How long have you been out here?" he asked.

"Fifteen minutes or so."

"Were you waiting for me to come home?"

The corners of her mouth turned up in an enigmatic smile. "How come you're home so early? Did all your friends get lucky and ditch you?"

For once, he wasn't in the mood to flirt. "I couldn't stop thinking about you," he said in all seriousness.

She hummed as if considering how to take this. Linc found himself taking off his jacket and reaching for his shirt buttons before he realized his intent.

"What are you doing?" she demanded as he stripped off his shirt, stepped out of his shoes and got to work on his pants.

"Joining you."

Her eyes widened as his pants fell to his ankles and he kicked out of them

"Don't you need a suit?"

In answer, he executed a shallow dive and surfaced ten feet beyond her. The shock of the cool water on his overheated skin diminished none of the desire pulsing through his veins. Three powerful strokes brought him within arm's reach of her and he wasted no time snagging her around the waist and dragging her flush against his body.

"Linc—" Her protest was cut off as he claimed her mouth in a hard kiss that let her know just how much he needed her.

She tasted like salt from the pool water and fresh peach pie with ice cream. He fed on her deliciousness with a ravenous appetite as she draped her thigh over his hip and gathered his wet hair between her fingers.

She rocked her pelvis into him and moaned. Peeling one strap of her bathing suit off her shoulder, he coasted his lips over her silky skin, enjoying the way she trembled.

"We shouldn't be doing this out here," she warned, her voice a husky rasp. She pushed weakly against his chest. "What if we're seen?"

"Stop worrying about that." He skimmed her bathing suit lower, baring one small breast. "I don't care if the whole world knows."

"You should," she gasped unsteadily.

Dipping his head, he pulled her tight nipple into his mouth and smiled as she shivered. For a long, heady moment, she was all pliant eagerness and he took complete advantage. But then she began shaking her head.

"Damn it, Linc." Her voice was a breathless moan as he nipped at her neck. "I'm trying to be sensible."

"There's no need."

"There's every need."

Hearing the solid conviction in her tone, he released a heartfelt sigh before peeling her hand off his bicep and kissing her palm. "Fine. But you need to know that I'm not a huge fan of sensible when it comes to you."

"I don't believe that's true. You are the most prudent and mindful man I've ever met."

Linc winced at her description of him, even though he knew it was true. His father had demonstrated what happens to a man who acts unwisely without considering the consequences to those around him. Linc would never do anything that would hurt his family or friends. He'd never expose Claire to what would surely be a scandal if they were caught.

"What if we skip all this sneaking around and just date? In public. Dinner. Dancing."

"Did you forget that I recently spent the day cooking so your mother could decide what to serve at the party she's throwing to introduce you to Charleston's most eligible females?"

"Fine," Linc grumbled. "I'll go to her party, and when I don't find anyone who suits me, will you be my date to the polo event next weekend?"

A breeze moved across the surface of the pool, agitating the illuminated water, casting shimmers of reflected light over Claire's damp skin. Shadows moved through her eyes as her hand came up and cupped his cheek.

"Take me upstairs and make love to me," she murmured, the words barely reaching his ears. "More than anything else, that's what I want."

Sensing it would do no good to push her further on the subject, Linc took her hand and drew her toward the stairs. She was giving him what she thought he needed. Physical companionship that made no demands on him. Well, that wasn't good enough, and it was about time he started convincing her that she deserved more and so did he.

Claire buried her face in a sweetly scented pillow and clung to a delicious dream. Linc's lips were moving along her neck while his fingers traced along her thigh toward her hip. This fantasy was familiar and reoccurred more frequently since he'd returned to Charleston after the baseball season. The more time she spent with Linc, the more treacherous her subconscious became. In the early morning hours before she slipped from her bed, he did incredible things to her body. She'd lost track of just how many times a climax had visited her with the dawn.

She moaned a little, trembling on the edge of wakefulness. Resisting the return to reality, she clung to the delicious sensations ranging across her sleep-warmed flesh. The contrast of his silky warm lips exploring her shoulder and the roughness of his beard aroused her, the light scrape of stubble against her skin awakening goose bumps all over her body.

For so long she'd immersed herself in scented lotions, sweet baby smells and gourmet meals for one. She hadn't wanted to acknowledge how much she'd missed the strength of a man's hands on her body, his wicked words whispered in her ears, telling her all the naughty things he wanted to do to her, the power of an orgasm she couldn't control.

"Now, this is a wonderful way to wake up," Linc murmured, his fingers lazily drifting over her abdomen before sliding lower.

Claire's eyes flashed opened. This wasn't a dream. She glanced around the dim room and spied the clock on the nightstand. It was shortly before six. Honey would still be sleeping. She could linger in this delicious fantasy a little while longer.

And yet it wasn't a dream. This was happening. The hand sliding between her legs to cup her belonged to a very real, very turned-on Linc. She clamped her eyes shut as a groan ripped from her throat. Panic smacked her hard in the chest, but that didn't stop her thighs from parting.

Her pulse began to race. All traces of sleepiness vanished beneath a rush of lust as his fingers traveled along her inner thigh, not quite making it to where she wanted him most.

"What are you doing to me?" She shifted her hips, rubbing against his morning erection, and was rewarded by his swift intake of breath followed by the bite of his fingers on her thigh, far from where she ached but near enough to cause her to groan.

"Yeah, that's the stuff." He kissed her ear, before taking the lobe between his teeth. The tiny flare of pain sent a rush of pleasure through her body.

"Linc." His name came out in a whimper, a plea for him to stop teasing her.

"What do you want?"

"Touch me."

"I am."

Her head thrashed on the pillow, hips gyrating as frustration built to a crescendo. "Not where I want you."

"And where is that?"

"Between my legs. I want to feel you inside me." She'd stopped feeling embarrassed about telling him what she needed. "Every part of me aches for you."

"That's my girl."

At last, his fingers glided into her core and she stopped breathing. She felt the lazy drift of his tongue against her neck as he circled her clit with an expert touch. The pressure was perfect and she surrendered to the building pleasure.

"You're so wet," he murmured, his low voice rumbling through her.

"You wake up hard," she teased breathlessly. "I wake up wet."

He paused. "All the time?"

From his tone, he was surprised. That made her smile. She reached back and hooked her arm around his neck, arching her body, offering him every part of her.

"When I'm dreaming about you." After last night, it made no sense to be cagey. She'd already revealed too much about how she felt.

"Does that happen often?" His hands stroked her with possessive expertise, claiming and demanding her surrender.

"Almost every night."

"Moan for me like you did last night," he whispered against her skin while pushing a finger inside her.

A kiss landed in the sensitive spot where her shoulder and neck came together. Claire's lips parted and she moaned as his finger started to move in and out of her.

"You are so soft. So perfect," he growled as she rocked her hips. "Yes, that's it. Show me how much you love this."

"Linc," she moaned again, but this time in protest. The building pressure warned her she was close. She grabbed his hand and sank her fingernails into his skin to let him know she meant business. "Not like this. I need you inside me."

He cursed softly and rolled away from her. Claire shifted onto her back and watched him find one of the foil packets. She briefly remembered how they hadn't used a condom last night before her mind snapped back to the present moment. To her delight, his hands shook a little as he tore it open and rolled the condom onto his erection.

And then he was sliding between her thighs and into her open arms, driving into her body with a groan that made her heart sing.

Claire clenched her eyes shut as Linc moved inside her, the better to savor the fullness of his possession. She'd never been particularly vocal during sex, but last night and now this morning, the urge to chant encouragement couldn't be denied.

"Yes, yes, yes. Please." She had no idea what she was asking for, but the pleas rolled off her tongue. "More. That feels amazing."

Her declaration ended on a gasp as he shifted the angle of his hips and changed his thrusts, going deeper, taking her pleasure higher.

"That's it," he coaxed, his voice raspy and gruff. "Show me what you like."

Had she ever felt like this before? Was it merely the years she'd gone without or did Linc have some sort of magic that made her wild?

"Oh, Linc."

They were moving together in a frenzy of hands and hips. Her body tightened with ever-increasing need until Claire wondered if she might explode. His name poured from her lips again and again, and she heard him murmuring encouragement as he thrust into her smoothly but with surging power.

And then she was coming, her orgasm catching up

with her so fast she wasn't ready for the blinding pleasure that blew her apart.

"You are perfect," he whispered. "I've never felt like this before."

With a final thrust, he let go and Claire watched his expression transform into something that both thrilled and terrified her. His lips claimed hers in a searing kiss that left her reeling. She clutched his hair and met the thrust of his tongue with desperation-fueled passion, recognizing that they couldn't keep doing this, yet she didn't want to stop. Being with Linc like this made her happier than she'd been in a long time. Maybe ever.

So what if it couldn't last. Nothing so perfect was meant to. She would simply have to take this time with him and appreciate every second. Being together, loving like this, wasn't hurting anyone. To hell with what the gossips said about them. Eventually their passion would run its course and Linc would find the woman he was meant to spend the rest of his life with.

As for what would happen to Claire…

She would just have to trust that he would treat her and Honey fairly.

"What are you thinking about?" Linc asked, his face buried in her neck.

"How nice it is to wake up with you."

He hummed. "I could get used to this."

She agreed. It would be so easy to lose herself in him. In this secret connection they shared. "You shouldn't."

His lips moved over her skin, and her breath quickened as dozens of nerve endings came to life.

How could she already want him again? Her body

hadn't calmed from the last orgasm he'd given her and she craved more of his touch. An ache bloomed between her thighs and she resisted the urge to rub herself against him.

"You're not the boss of me," he teased, his lips coasting along the curve of her breast, tongue flicking over her nipple, making her suck in a sharp breath.

"Of course not." She arched her back, offering herself to him. "That's your mother's job."

He lifted his head and snagged her gaze. The blue of his eyes seemed to intensify. "I'm my own man. I make my own decisions."

"Of course you do."

Her teasing was distracting him from the romantic mood he'd been in a moment earlier. She breathed a little sigh of relief. Passionate Linc she could handle. Sex was a physical act. She might crave it, hunger for his lips on her and the heat of their lovemaking, but when things ended, her heart would still be intact. Affectionate Linc was trouble. She could come to depend on his smiles and ache for his company.

"You're patronizing me."

"I wouldn't dream of it." She tunneled her fingers in his soft golden hair, enjoying its silky feel. "It's just that you don't really belong only to yourself. You're a star. A hero."

He shook his head. "I'm no one's hero."

Why didn't he see himself as everyone else did? Didn't he realize the impact he had on his friends and family?

"The decisions you make affect the people around you," she told him.

"What happens between us doesn't affect anyone outside this bed."

"Have you forgotten your mother?"

He blinked at her. "Please tell me you didn't just bring her into this."

"She wants you involved with the sort of quality woman you can eventually marry. Don't you want to make her happy?"

Linc flopped onto his back and stared at the ceiling. "This is without a doubt the strangest post-sex conversation I've ever had with a woman."

"I'm just looking out for you."

He shifted his gaze back to her. "Maybe you should stop worrying about me and consider what makes you happy."

Claire opened her mouth to say that she was doing just that but shook her head instead. Since finding out she was pregnant with Honey, she'd put her daughter first. Honey's security and happiness was all that mattered. This interlude with Linc had been selfish and reckless. Claire's throat closed as panic enveloped her.

"I shouldn't be here," she whispered, sitting up and looking around for her clothes. "I'm so sorry."

"Why are you apologizing?" Linc made a grab for her arm, but she'd already slipped out of the bed. "Claire, don't go."

"It's late. Honey will be getting up soon and I have to start your breakfast." She knew she was babbling, but she had to remind herself what was important. "You're supposed to be at the gym for your workout."

"I already had my morning workout."

His tone was so smoky she couldn't resist glancing at him. Her heart gave a start as he slipped off the bed and stood naked before her. The sheer perfection of his chiseled torso, powerful thighs and sleep-tossed hair made her knees weak and her blood started to pound in her ears. If he reached for her, she'd fall back into his arms without a moment's hesitation.

"That was cardio," she retorted, tearing her eyes from him. "You need to balance it with lifting and…"

The rest was lost as he grabbed her around the waist and hauled her up against him. He set his fingers beneath her chin and tilted her head to the perfect angle. She melted against his solid form as his lips claimed hers in a possessive kiss. Her tongue darted forward to tangle with his and she moaned as he palmed her butt cheek and lifted her against his growing erection. She dug her fingers into his shoulders and hung on as he feasted on her mouth. The rest of the world fell away, leaving her trapped in a whirlpool where only his hard muscles, strong hands and passionate mouth kept her grounded.

By the time he broke the kiss and gazed down at her dazed expression, she was weak with desire. Whatever he wanted to do to her, she would've gladly said yes. He surveyed her bruised lips and brushed his knuckles lightly against her tight nipples, satisfaction plain in his half smile.

"I'm going to take you and Honey out for breakfast," he announced. "You have half an hour to get ready."

Before she could protest that she wasn't recovered enough from their morning activity to be seen in public with him, he turned her toward the door and gave her a friendly pat on her rear end. She was in the hallway before her brain could form a coherent thought and by then he'd disappeared into his master bathroom.

After checking on Honey and finding her still sleeping, Claire decided she would take a cold shower and restore her equilibrium. If this was to work with Linc, she had to figure out how to give him everything in the bedroom while giving nothing away outside of it. It was a tricky path to walk, but if she wanted this time with him, she would just have to make it work.

Eight

The morning of his mother's party, Linc woke alone in his bed with a sense of foreboding. These past few nights with Claire had been some of the best he'd ever known. Her passion and openness drove him to want to take her pleasure higher each time they made love.

And she'd surprised him by being a curious and sensitive partner in bed, up for any number of adventurous activities. The shyness she often demonstrated vanished behind his closed bedroom door and this intrigued Linc all the more.

One thing she hadn't given him was any deeper insight into the hopes, fears and dreams that had shaped the woman she'd become. As much as he'd spoken of how things had been before and after his father's illegal dealings had surfaced, she'd glossed over her own childhood experiences growing up in San Francisco, leaving him with a vague picture of a little girl who'd been lonely and neglected by her father after her mother had left them.

Nor had he had any luck bringing their relationship into the light of day. As soon as the sun came up, she returned to her housekeeper role. He'd made no headway on breaching the walls she erected that kept him at a professional distance.

Which was why when he found her in his kitchen, going over her to-do lists for his mother's party, he decided to tackle what was bothering him.

"This upstairs-downstairs thing with you isn't working for me."

She regarded him blankly. "The what?"

"You and I have a connection. I want more than just a sexual relationship with you."

For a moment, she had the audacity to grin at him, but when he continued to regard her in all seriousness, she sobered. "I get what you're trying to say, but it's the way things have to be."

"I don't like it."

"Be realistic, Linc. You can't trot me out as the woman you're sleeping with—"

"Seeing."

She made a face and shook her head. "Because I will never fit in."

"That's not true. Not one of my friends gives a damn who I choose to date as long as I'm happy."

She cocked her head. "Really? So they supported you marrying London?"

He considered his conversation with Knox. "That's different. They were worried that she wasn't right for me."

Claire's expression said it all.

Linc snorted in disgust. "Not because she wasn't from an old Charleston family, but because they weren't sure she loved me."

"Has it occurred to you that they're going to be even more skeptical of my motives? London has a lot of money and she runs a successful business. She's a gorgeous trendsetter and well connected. I'm your *housekeeper*." Claire's expression twisted into disgust. "We're nothing but a cliché. They are going to see me as nothing more than an opportunist."

"Not once they get to know you."

She shook her head. "I won't fit in."

"You don't even want to try."

"You're right. I'm afraid." Color spilled into Claire's cheeks. "One of the things I'm terrible at is standing up for myself. I can't tell you how many times I've let people bully me." She paused and met his gaze with eyes as hard as granite. "This town is elitist, judgmental and cliquey. Why would you want to be with a woman who won't fit in?"

It was on the tip of his tongue to insist that he didn't care when he realized that didn't matter. Claire cared. For her own peace of mind as well as for his reputation and how this would affect his mother.

"I wish you could trust me," he said after a short pause. The throb in his voice made her flinch.

"It's not a matter of trusting you." But she didn't sound convincing.

From the little she'd shared about her past, he was pretty sure that every time she needed to rely on someone, that person had come up short. He thought of what had happened to his mother when Linc's dad had first gone to prison and then divorced her. What if Linc and Sawyer hadn't been there with their love and support, making a tough time a little easier?

Often Linc had thought it odd that Claire had moved to Charleston and put the entire width of the country between her and her family. Maybe she didn't have anyone who made her life easier or better.

"I'd never do anything to hurt you," he told her.

"I'm not worried about that." She sucked in a lungful of air and then expelled it on a harsh sigh. "It's not you I don't trust, it's me. Sometimes I don't protect myself well enough and get hurt because of it. I know you aren't going to hurt me. It's not in your nature. But you can't control everyone or everything."

He was starting to understand her concerns. "So it's okay for us to keep sleeping together as long as no one finds out."

"For now. It's working for both of us at the moment." She shrugged. "When that changes, it will mean a cleaner finish if we keep things in perspective."

Basically, what she was saying was that she didn't want to get emotionally entangled with him. He'd been right to think that she wasn't over her late husband. And wasn't he the perfect guy for her to take up with? In her mind, their relationship had a built-in countdown. A few weeks. Maybe a month. Some palate-cleansing sex for him. A bridge between London and the next woman he became seriously involved with.

Linc wanted to punch something. This wasn't what he'd signed up for when he pursued Claire, but it seemed that it was all she intended to offer.

"How very practical of you," he said. "I guess I'd better head to the gym and get my workout in before the party."

After waiting a heartbeat for her to say something more, Linc realized she'd emptied her conversational basket of all its goodies and he would get nothing else. Turning on his heel, he exited the kitchen.

By the time he returned home, Claire was gone and the house had the same empty feeling it always did when she and Honey were out. Funny how he didn't get the same vibe in his Fort Worth home. Maybe because his housekeeper there didn't live-in, so her presence in the house didn't have any impact one way or another. Or perhaps because during baseball season his head was filled with the game and he had little downtime to notice that he was lonely.

Knowing his mother would be on edge before the party, Linc made sure he was at her house half an hour early. She received him in her bedroom, where she was having her makeup done. Sawyer had also arrived and was sitting on the chaise in the corner, watching their mother's transformation. She winked at him as he entered.

Bettina waved her hand. "Come over here so I can get a look at you."

Linc did as he was asked. Tonight, he'd donned a navy suit with a white shirt and bright blue-striped tie. When he'd chosen the latter, he'd imagined Claire smiling up at him as she commented how the blue matched his eyes.

"Do I meet with your approval?" he teased, seeing his mother's fond smile.

"You make me proud." Her gaze flashed toward her daughter, who wore a figure-hugging black dress that bared her toned legs and arms. Bettina frowned. "There's still time before the party if you want to run home and change," she told Sawyer. "To put on something with a little more color maybe."

"I like what I'm wearing." In one smooth move, Sawyer got to her feet and headed for the door. "Besides, Linc is the one everyone is going to be focused on tonight. No one will even notice I'm here."

Before their mother could do more than snort her disapproval, Sawyer vanished through the door. Linc stared after her in amusement. At least until her words penetrated.

Everyone would be focused on him tonight. He was the main event.

Normally this would appeal to him, but the idea that most of the women attending the party had their sights set on becoming his wife meant he would be disappointing a lot of people over the course of the evening.

"I'm going to go grab a drink," he murmured, setting his hands on his mother's shoulders and meeting her gaze in the mirror. "You look beautiful."

"Don't drink too much. Remember, this party is a marathon, not a sprint."

"But I'm such a happy drunk," he teased.

In fact, he held his liquor very well and tended to quit earlier than most of his friends. The last thing he needed was to get caught in a compromising situation because he'd drunk to excess and have his exploits splashed all over social media.

His mother regarded him in mock sternness. "We're trying to make a good impression here."

"Everyone finds me charming and irresistible. I'll be fighting them off by the end of the evening."

"I hope so. Not everyone in this town is convinced you are a good catch."

Linc could see this bothered his mother and thought he understood why. "I don't care what people think and you'd be a lot happier if you didn't, either. There are a lot of small-minded people who believe their social position gives them the right to judge others. The same people who were happy standing on the shoulders of those less fortunate when Daddy roped them into his Ponzi scheme are the ones who think they're better than him. But they behaved just as badly."

"Your father made things hard for all of us."

"Which is why you should be so proud of everything you accomplished."

His mother's expression became uncharacteristically bleak. "What did I do besides keep a roof over your heads and put food on the table? Even that was a struggle until you started pitching in." Bettina shook her head. "And don't think for one second that I don't realize my blind desire for social prominence is what prompted me to marry your father. If I hadn't been so focused on the Thurston name, I might have chosen a man with integrity. Instead, I took someone without a lick of sense and made him think he had to take idiotic risks to further our social standing."

Linc hated hearing his mother take the blame for his father's bad judgment. "He chose to rely on shortcuts instead of hard work."

"He was never all that ambitious."

Which was why after getting out of prison, he'd divorced Bettina and married an outsider with a lot of money.

"You know, it was your belief in me that made me such a success. And what about Sawyer? She's a driving force for conservation in this city. Do you think she would have the passion for preserving Charleston's history if not for the stories you told us growing up?"

"You two are my joy. I want the best for you."

Linc gave his mother's shoulders a gentle squeeze. "I know."

"That's why I threw this party, so you could meet some suitable women."

His mother hadn't yet asked what was going on between him and Claire, but he suspected she would if he didn't go on a date with one or more of tonight's guests. "Go check on Claire and see how she's doing," his mother said. "I want everything to be perfect tonight."

"I'm sure she has everything in hand, but I'll see if she needs anything."

Downstairs, Linc poked his head into the kitchen and

found a completely unflustered Claire giving instructions to her waitstaff. Determining she had everything under control, he went in search of Sawyer and found her chatting with the bartender setting up in the sunporch off the main living room.

"Hey," Linc said, eyeing the drink in Sawyer's hand. "Starting already?"

"Not that it's any of your business, but it's club soda." She sipped the drink and changed the subject. "Are you sure it was a good idea inviting all your friends tonight?"

"Absolutely." Linc had hoped to redistribute some of the pressure the female guests were sure to bring. All his friends were single and one perfect girl away from settling down. "Austin, Knox and Roy have been looking for some new meat."

Sawyer made a face. "Yuck."

"You say that, but I bet every one of them hooks up tonight."

"Challenge accepted," she said, an adversarial glint in her eye. "I will make it my solemn duty to warn everyone in here about your buddies."

The idea that Sawyer would be running around cockblocking his friends amused Linc. "They're not all bad," he said, testing out a theory. "Knox, for example, is a great guy."

"He's no better than the rest."

Even though he watched his sister carefully, she gave no sign that corroborated his suspicions that she was into his best friend. Time to push a little harder. "That's not true. In fact, I think he's seriously interested in someone."

"Why do you say that?" Sawyer looked only mildly curious.

"Because from what I can tell, he hasn't taken a girl back to his place since I returned to Charleston and there are a lot of nights he doesn't come out with us at all."

Sawyer waved her hand, dismissing his theory. "That doesn't mean he's interested in someone. Maybe he's really busy or just sick of hanging out and drinking every night with a bunch of thirtysomething adolescents."

Linc shook his head. "There's more to it than that. I know my friend. The only time he isn't looking to hook up is when he's already involved."

"You're imagining things."

"Sort of like you," he said, hoping this time he could trip her up and she'd admit she was seeing someone. Someone like Knox.

"Sort of like me what?"

"I think you're dating someone. I've put Knox on your trail. It's only a matter of time before he figures out who it is and tells me."

Sawyer frowned at him in puzzlement. "Why do you care?"

"I need to set the guy straight about you." Linc liked playing the part of the protective big brother. He'd assumed the role as soon as Sawyer started kindergarten. "It's important that he knows if he breaks your heart, I'm going to kick his ass."

"Nice," she scoffed, her voice dry. "You don't need to

worry. No one is going to break my heart, and besides, what if he's bigger than you and kicks your ass instead?"

Linc snorted. At six feet two inches of solid muscle, he wasn't worried. "Yeah, that's not going to happen."

"It's not going to happen because it doesn't need to happen." Sawyer set her empty glass down and indicated she wanted a refill. "You don't need to watch out for me. I'm a big girl."

"But it's my job to take care of you and Mom."

Their dad sure as hell hadn't been around to do that, even before his financial schemes landed him in jail.

"That's sweet," Sawyer said. "Worry about Mom all you want, but I can take care of myself just fine."

"Okay, then answer me this. Are you dating anyone?"

"Shouldn't you be greeting your guests or something?"

"Nobody's here yet."

"Then why don't you go pester Claire? Or bug this guy to make sure the bar is stocked with the right kind of bourbon."

"Why don't you answer my question?" Both her expression and her silence told Linc he would get nowhere. That didn't stop him from persisting. "Have you ever considered dating Knox?"

"I thought you said he was already interested in someone."

"What if that someone is you?"

Sawyer's eyes went wide and she gave her head a vigorous shake. "Me and your best friend? That's a recipe for disaster."

"I disagree. You two have a lot in common with your love of preserving Charleston's old buildings. I figure if he ever decides to settle down, you'd be good for him."

"What about him being good for me?"

"You're right." Linc knew his sister well enough to recognize when it was time to back off. While he believed she and Knox would be a perfect match, too much pushing from him and they'd never realize it. "Forget I said anything."

Sawyer was quiet for a long time, but Linc held his tongue and waited her out. In the end, his patience was rewarded.

"You're right that we do have a lot in common."

"Do you want me to have him ask you out?"

"Geez, Linc. No. Forget it. Don't you dare say anything to him."

"Too late. I've already put the idea in his head."

"Linc Thurston, how dare you meddle in my love life."

"To quote our mother, 'I just want you to be happy.'"

"Then you'll mind your own business and never speak of this again."

"You know I can't do that. I inherited our mother's meddling gene."

To his surprise, Sawyer wrapped her arms around his neck and gave him a fierce hug. "Everything is going to be all right with both of us," she murmured. "You'll see."

Linc put his arms around her and squeezed gently in return, basking in her affection. "I hope you're right."

But all he could think about was the endless party

that stretched before him and how a certain brunette with soulful brown eyes was going to handle seeing dozens of women flirting with him all evening long. He only hoped she'd hate it as much as he was going to.

Carrying a stack of clean plates, Claire scanned Bettina's party guests and the waitstaff and the bartenders, making sure everything was running smoothly. In addition to sending Jenny and Steve around with trays of appetizers and glasses of wine, Claire had opted to set up hors d'oeuvres in a couple locations. Every fifteen minutes or so, she made a loop of the party.

It might have seemed like she was micromanaging things, but staying focused on the tasks at hand kept her from dwelling on all the beautiful women in attendance and wondering which of them would end up with Linc. Automatically, her gaze swept the room in search of him. Her chest ached when she spied him in a group composed of his friends and a familiar blonde woman. Everly Briggs looked comfortable and at home as she repeatedly touched Linc's arm as if to punctuate whatever she was saying.

Although Claire had seen a significant number of women vying for Linc's attention tonight, for some reason, seeing him with Everly made her feel slightly sick. Perhaps it was because the woman had been so forward at the grocery store. And even though she suspected it had been more curiosity than cruelty that had made the woman so blunt, Claire couldn't help but feel uneasy at her appearance here tonight. Would she be bold enough to repeat to Linc the gossip she'd shared with Claire?

"Claire, are you all right?" Jenny asked, pulling her attention away from Everly and Linc. The waitress stood beside her with a tray of dirty glasses and plates.

"I'm fine," Claire said as she surreptitiously indicated Everly. "I ran into that blonde woman standing next to Linc a few weeks ago at the grocery store and made the mistake of telling her I worked for him. Do you know anything about her?"

"Everly Briggs? She's big on the charity circuit."

"That makes sense. She wanted to hire me to do an event. What does she do?"

"She owns some sort of branding company." Jenny lowered her voice. "There was a huge scandal involving her sister last year. She went to jail after leaking a bunch of engineering documents or something to her employer's competitor. I heard they were worth over two million dollars."

"Why would she do that?"

"Apparently, she thought she was going to get fired and wanted to get back at the company before that happened. Plus, she thought it would help her get a job with the competitor."

That Jenny knew so much of the story didn't surprise Claire at all. She'd heard snatches of several tales tonight as she moved through the crowd. This group of people seemed to feed off drama and loved to share every juicy tidbit.

"Well, that's just crazy," Claire said. "Why would she think that was a good idea?"

"I don't know. Maybe crazy runs in the family."

"Should I warn Linc?" He didn't need someone like that in his life.

"Naw," Jenny said, sliding a sidelong glance in Claire's direction. "I don't think she's Linc's type."

Her friend's sly grin caught Claire off guard, but she quickly recovered. "I wasn't wondering that."

"Sure."

"I wasn't." Claire gave her head a little toss. "Although, I think he could do better."

"Well, he certainly has plenty to choose from at this party. I wonder if he enjoys all the attention or if he finds it irritating."

"Most men would love to be fawned over by all these women," Claire said. "On the other hand, Bettina has made it clear that she's hosting this party so he can meet some eligible women and possibly start a relationship with one of them. I imagine he has to feel a little bit like prey."

The two women went their own way, Jenny to deliver the dirty dishes to the kitchen and Claire to continue making sure the party was going smoothly. She greeted several of Linc's friends as she passed them. Apparently, Linc hadn't wanted to face the horde of marriage-minded women without backup. Claire spied Knox deep in conversation with Sawyer and wondered if those two had ever tried dating or if Linc didn't trust his baby sister with his best friend.

After checking on the inventory behind the portable bar set up in the parlor and finding satisfactory levels of alcohol and mix, she retreated into the kitchen to assess the situation there.

"How are we doing?" she asked Trudy, the woman she'd hired to assist her with the preparations. "Anything we're running low on?"

"Your crab puffs are a huge hit. Good thing we made more than you originally planned."

Claire nodded. "This is a town that likes its seafood."

With a large party like this, so many things could go wrong, but she'd been planning and organizing like a fiend. Over the next few hours, things went so smoothly it was almost anticlimactic. By ten o'clock, she estimated a third of the party guests had taken off. With the gathering winding down, all she had left to do was clean up and head out.

While she collected trays and chafing dishes from the buffet, Claire surreptitiously looked around for Linc, curious if he'd found someone he wanted to spend some quiet one-on-one time with. Throughout the evening, every time she'd ventured through the room, he'd been conversing with a different woman. His mother had to be thrilled that he was taking her matchmaking so seriously.

As if her thoughts had summoned him, Linc came up beside her. His long, warm fingers curved around her arm, and he gave her a brief heart-wrenching squeeze.

"Another successful event under your belt. Your food is fantastic and pretty soon everyone in Charleston is going to know who you are."

His praise and support made Claire light-headed. "I'm sure they already know I'm your housekeeper."

"I'm talking about the polo match that's coming up.

You'll make a huge splash as the caterer and I'm sure my mother would be happy to talk you up to her friends."

"You know, it sounds like you're trying to get rid of me."

"Not at all. It's just that several people have mentioned to me lately that your talents are going to waste as my housekeeper. I thought maybe your loyalty to me might be stopping you from starting your own catering business." Though he smiled as he said it, his blue eyes were grave.

"I'd never do that." Her throat tightened at the thought of leaving him. "I don't have the money or the know-how to start my own company."

"But if you did?"

Although she was flattered that so many people had faith in her cuisine, the pressure to succeed overwhelmed her. "I also don't have the time or the desire. You know that Honey is my top priority. Also, there are so many well-established caterers in Charleston, I can't imagine being able to compete." She offered him a wry smile. "So it looks like you're stuck with me."

To her relief, the corner of his mouth kicked up in a matching grin. "That's good to hear, but I don't want to stand in your way if you think doing something else might be better for you and Honey."

"I know it must seem that I'm unambitious, but I'm happy right where I am." The position enabled her to stay below the radar and out of sight of Jasper's parents. "So, have you picked one yet?" she asked, deciding to change the subject.

"Picked one?" he echoed with a slight frown.

She used her chin to indicate the crowd. Hadn't he noticed the way all eyes had been following him tonight? Every single woman here, with the exception of Sawyer, had her sights set on becoming Mrs. Lincoln Thurston.

"Your mother and sister have delivered every eligible female in Charleston to your doorstep. All you need to do is choose."

"Truthfully, they all look the same to me. Not one of them stands out as someone I want to get to know." He sighed.

"You haven't given any of them a chance," Claire said, secretly hoping that it would take him a while to settle on just one. For the moment, she liked having him all to herself. "You should pick three tonight and invite each of them out for dinner."

Linc's blue eyes glinted with irritation. "I can't believe you're okay with this."

"I'm a realist." Claire hoped her voice didn't betray the lie. "It's what has to happen."

"It doesn't have to happen this way."

"You know that it does. You might have been okay marrying a woman your mother didn't approve of, but I'll bet it was hard on London knowing Bettina would never fully welcome her."

Before she'd finished speaking, a lovely blonde appeared at Linc's side and wrapped her hand around his arm in a possessive gesture. From what Claire had observed, Charleston seemed to have an overabundance of slender, elegant blonde women with perfect teeth and fine manners. She almost pitied Linc having to choose one, because none had stood out for her and she couldn't imagine him settling for a woman who was interchangeable with a dozen others.

"There you are," the newcomer said, behaving as if Linc had been having a conversation with thin air. "I've been dying for a chance to catch up with you all night, but you've been surrounded."

Although Claire expected to be treated as if she didn't exist, Linc wasn't the sort to play along. Claire had noticed that he gave everyone his full attention, treating them like they mattered. From the gardener who maintained the meticulous landscaping around the Jonathan Elliot House to the mailman and his neighbor's dog walker.

"Phoebe Reed," he said, gesturing toward Claire, "this is Claire Robbins. She is responsible for all the delicious food."

Forced to be polite, the blonde tore her rapt gaze from Linc and glanced in Claire's direction, giving her a perfunctory nod. "I'm sure it's all quite yummy." Minor courtesy out of the way, she returned her full attention to Linc. "Your sister tells me you're going to be a part of the holiday home tour. I can't wait to see what you've done to the Jonathan Elliot House."

Rather than be an awkward third wheel, Claire murmured, "I have to get back to the kitchen." And before Linc could stop her, she faded into the dwindling crowd.

As much as she wanted to dwell on Phoebe and the dozen other beautiful, wealthy, socially connected women who'd been brought here with the purpose of getting acquainted with Linc, Claire had a job to do.

Taking up one of the big trays she'd brought from the kitchen, she moved around the room, collecting empty dishes and glasses. The guests thinned out more still as she worked.

She was making her third round of the rooms when someone spoke from just behind her. "Hello." The cultured female voice sounded familiar. "It's Claire, right?"

Claire turn to face Everly Briggs and her stomach dropped.

"Yes," Claire said cautiously, with a polite smile fixed on her lips. "And you're Everly."

She was dying to ask how the woman knew Bettina, but she figured Everly fell into the same category as most of the women attending the party: Charleston social elite.

"I hear you were in charge of the food tonight. I just knew you were talented."

The woman's enthusiasm wasn't winning Claire over. Something about their encounter at the grocery store and the assumptions Everly had made, followed by her appearance tonight, left Claire feeling uneasy.

"Thank you." She glanced to the side, hoping Everly would take the hint and let Claire get about her task.

"I suppose you're a little surprised to see me here," Everly continued, relaxing into the conversation and missing Claire's subtle signal.

"A little." Claire told herself to let it go, but curiosity had a mind of its own. Maybe if she hadn't heard about Everly's sister from Jenny, she wouldn't have cared. After all, in certain circles, most everyone in Charleston was connected in one way or another. "From our last conversation, I got the impression you didn't know Linc."

"I don't. I tagged along with a friend of mine, Augusta Hobbs." Everly gave Claire a conspiratorial smile. "Although we've been at several of the same events, I've never actually met Linc. Turns out he's as wonderful as you said."

Had Claire described Linc as wonderful?

"I can see why you'd enjoy working for him," the woman continued. "He's very genuine. As well as handsome and wealthy. How have you managed to be around him all the time and not fall in love?"

Claire felt herself flushing beneath the woman's keen regard, but she kept her gaze and voice cool as she said, "He's my boss."

Everly smirked. "Yes, I know, but haven't you fantasized about him even a little?"

"No." Once again, their conversation was straying to inappropriate topics. Cheeks hot, Claire regarded the woman with a flat stare before she found her voice again. "If you'll excuse me, I still have a lot to do."

"Of course, but before you go, I was wondering if we could meet for lunch early next week to discuss the food for the charity polo match."

The request seemed to come from out of the blue. "Are you involved with the event?"

"Yes. I wasn't able to make the meeting last week with Genevieve and Portia when they asked you to cater the event. I'm in charge of the food and wanted to discuss the menu with you."

Claire wished Everly had led with that instead of

talking about Linc. She relaxed a little. "Of course. When would you like to do that?"

"Could you meet on Monday or Tuesday?"

"How about Tuesday. Would one o'clock work?"

"One o'clock would be perfect. Why don't I meet you at Magnolias."

"That would be fine. Now, I really need to get back to the kitchen," Claire said, pretending she'd seen something that needed her attention. Instinct urged her to get away from this woman.

"Looking forward to our meeting on Tuesday." Everly's drawl pursued Claire as she fled.

Nine

The morning following his mother's party, Linc was summoned to her house for a debriefing. She wanted his opinion of the women he'd met and some indication that he intended to date one or two of them.

When he arrived, Bettina was at her dining room table, eating a poached egg with toast and fresh fruit. She liked her coffee dark and rich with liberal splashes of cream and instructed Dolly to pour him a cup before he sat down.

"I thought last night's party went quite well," his mother said without preamble. "Lyla Madison's daughter is quite accomplished and has the sort of beauty that ages well."

"Which one was she?" he asked, thanking Dolly with a smile as he accepted a delicate china cup.

"The brunette in pink. She's a CPA at the accounting firm I use." Bettina frowned as Linc continued to regard her blankly. "You spoke with her for half an hour."

"Sorry. There were so many women there. I lost track of names."

"Linc, I need you to take this seriously." Bettina let her gaze rest on him for a long moment before speaking again. "You simply must marry someone from our social circles."

As much as Linc hated to disappoint his mother, he needed to get something off his chest. "What if I fall in love with someone who isn't from an old Charleston family?"

"Have you?"

Confronted by his mother's demand, Linc found himself hesitating.

"Is this about Claire?" Bettina continued. "I've seen how you are with her. But she's your housekeeper."

"I don't care."

His mother huffed. "You're acting like your father, doing something without considering the consequences."

"I'm nothing like my father," he retorted through gritted teeth.

"I'll admit you haven't behaved like him before this." Bettina tossed her napkin onto her half-finished breakfast. "Honestly, Linc. Have you thought any of this through? You have a social position—"

"You've never accepted that I don't care about that." He'd come here today expecting resistance, but he wasn't prepared to defend his future with Claire, because he hadn't figured out what he wanted.

"Then what do you care about?"

"I care about Claire."

"That's all well and good..." His mother regarded him in exasperation. "And I've always said my children's happiness is my top priority, but—"

"She makes me happy." Linc was firm on that. "She's an amazing woman and a terrific mother. We have this amazing chemistry, and I'm happier spending time with her and Honey than with anyone else on the planet." His voice grew stronger with each sentence.

"So what are you planning to do? Marry Claire and become Honey's father?" Bettina demanded, her tone skeptical. "Is that what she wants?"

Linc would be lying if he said he had everything figured out, but now that the question had been asked, the answer was clear. "I think that's where we're headed. And if anyone has anything negative to say about that or her, they will have me to contend with."

His mother narrowed her eyes and regarded him for several seconds before nodding. "When you put it that way, of course I'll accept Claire."

"Just like that?" Linc couldn't help being suspicious of his mother's abrupt capitulation. "After everything you said about London's lack of a social pedigree, you're suddenly okay with me being in a relationship with my housekeeper?"

"You never fought for London." It was less a statement of fact and more of an accusation.

Leave it to Bettina to twist things around until Linc didn't know if he was coming or going.

"I shouldn't have had to."

"Regardless." Disapproval tightened his mother's mouth. "You never championed her."

Linc couldn't understand where she was coming from. "What does that matter? London was strong and could take care of herself."

"Are you saying Claire isn't as strong?"

"She may not always defend herself, but she will do whatever it takes to keep Honey safe."

"I agree about Claire, but I think you're wrong about London. She needed you to be there, but you weren't. I kept waiting for you to stand up for her, and when you never did, I knew she wasn't the woman for you."

Linc studied his mother while he processed her statement. "Are you telling me London's outsider status didn't bother you? You were just using it to test if I was willing to fight for our love?"

"Exactly."

"So you wanted me to convince you I was madly in love with her?"

"And you never did," his mother said. "I never believed London was the most important woman in your life and neither did she. That's what kept her from feeling secure in your relationship. What made her so needy and controlling."

Was that true? Had he let London down? What his mother said made sense. He and London had been engaged for two years without committing to a wedding date. She'd tried pinning him down several times and each time he came up with an excuse for why he wasn't ready. Was it because with each passing month, he'd grown less and less confident that she was the right woman for him?

Would he eventually feel that way about Claire?

Linc couldn't imagine a time that he wouldn't want to be with her. In fact, with each hour they spent apart, he grew more impatient to have her all to himself. Was that love? He'd certainly never felt like this with London.

And what if Claire didn't feel the same way about him? She'd made it pretty clear all she was interested in was a casual physical relationship. Was that what she'd told him because she didn't believe he could ever want more? Or because she hadn't stopped grieving for her late husband?

One thing he was certain of, after the polo match event, they were going to have a serious discussion about taking their relationship public. His conversation with his mother today had made it clear that the only way Claire was going to believe they had a future was if he demonstrated he was going to fight for one.

After spending a fun morning with Honey and Linc at the aquarium, Claire was not in the mood for a business lunch with Everly Briggs. But she'd committed to doing the food for the polo event and Everly was the one in charge.

Claire dressed for the meeting in a blue-and-white seersucker shirtdress with short sleeves and a belt. She'd bought the dress at a consignment shop she'd found near Meeting and George Street and liked how the style was both professional and feminine.

When she arrived at the restaurant, Everly wasn't yet

there. The hostess showed Claire to a table beneath an enormous painting of a magnolia blossom. While the exposed ceiling beams and pine floors gave the space an industrial feel, the white tablecloths and metal vines corkscrewing up the iron support posts added sophistication. Claire was pondering the squat crystal vase with sprigs of tiny white flowers in the middle of the table when her lunch companion arrived.

"You're early," Everly said as she sat down opposite Claire. "I can't tell you how much that impresses me. So many people don't value another person's time. Where is your daughter? I was looking forward to seeing her again."

"I left her home. We went to the aquarium this morning and she's pretty tired out." Claire wondered why Everly thought she'd bring Honey. "And this is a business lunch, after all. It didn't seem appropriate to bring her."

"Of course. Is she with Linc Thurston? I heard he took her to the children's museum a week ago." Everly looked delighted. "How nice for you to have a built-in babysitter."

Claire fought against rising panic. "He was just helping me out the one time because I was catering his mother's party." Although in truth, it had happened several times. Linc was someone who needed to keep busy, and for him, spending time with a toddler was anything but boring. Plus, not having to keep an eye on Honey freed Claire to tackle some projects that were challenging with a toddler around.

"Don't worry," Everly said with a toothy smile that

didn't quite reach her eyes. "I wouldn't dream of saying anything."

"The food here looks so good. Do you have anything you recommend?"

Everly languidly waved her hand. "It's all good."

As soon as the women ordered lunch, Claire got down to business. She didn't like this woman and refused to linger over the meal any longer than absolutely necessary. But Everly had a different agenda.

"With your accent, you obviously aren't from the South," the blonde woman began, her bright green eyes fixed on Claire as if she was the most fascinating person in the room. "Where is your family from?"

Although the last thing Claire wanted to do was talk about herself, she imagined that parting with a few details would be okay.

"I grew up in California, the Bay Area. San Francisco." Claire added this last detail because she'd found some people in Charleston acted as if little beyond South Carolina was worth knowing about.

"I've never been to San Francisco, but I understand there's a lot of fine dining there. Is that why you became a chef?"

No need to explain that her father hadn't been the sort to take her out for fancy dinners. Or that she'd waitressed all through high school and became fascinated by everything that went on in the kitchen.

"I grew up watching cooking shows and started experimenting with recipes when I was nine."

"I imagine your mother appreciated the help in the

kitchen. Are you looking forward to sharing your love of food with your daughter?"

Actually, her mother had left shortly after Claire turned seven and her father hadn't been all that good in the kitchen. So if she wanted something more than canned spaghetti and hot dogs, she'd realized she needed to learn how to cook.

"Honey is already showing signs of being an excellent chef," Claire said.

"Is your husband a chef as well?"

Claire kept her smile in place, but her irritation was growing. "No, actually he was in the military."

"I see." Everly's nod seemed to indicate that explained something. "Is he stationed nearby?"

"No." Claire stared at her water glass to avoid meeting Everly's gaze. She hated how everyone reacted when she spoke of what had happened to Jasper. "He was killed in action several years ago."

"Oh, that's just terrible. I'm so sorry. What a shame that Honey will never get to know her father."

"Yes. Well…" Claire trailed off into uncomfortable silence. She was used to people's condolences, but this conversation was more of an interview than idle lunch chatter. "Unfortunately, she wasn't the only child who lost her father that day."

"So you moved all the way across the country to Charleston. That's a big step. Don't you miss your family?"

"I wanted to start fresh," Claire said, keeping her answer vague. "Charleston has an interesting history and it's quite lovely."

She had no intention of sharing the story of her family connection to one of the state's founding families. Chances were it was just some bit of nonsense made up by one of her ancestors. Back in the 1800s, with travel being so arduous and a Civil War brewing between the North and the South, it would've been virtually impossible to prove someone's claim of being the second son of a wealthy well-connected family.

And even if the story was true, Claire couldn't imagine some long lost relatives opening their arms to welcome a stranger into their exclusive group, especially one who'd grown up in California.

Deciding to take control of the conversation, Claire cleared her throat and said, "Can you tell me a little bit about the food you arranged with the former caterer for your polo event? Is it a buffet or a sit-down lunch?"

Everly hesitated before answering, looking like she was reluctant to get down to business. At last, she gave a little flutter of her fingers and began. "The way we bring in revenue at this event is by selling tickets to the match and also offering special baskets for lunch. We've had a hundred baskets preordered. Each one costs three hundred dollars and will feed two people."

Claire nodded as she jotted notes on a small pad of paper. She'd done a little research on the sorts of food served at a polo match. She intended to propose a sampler of sandwiches made with beef, ham, perhaps salmon, definitely one of vegetables. An artisanal meat and cheese tray with a delectable kale salad or perhaps a cold soup, maybe both. And seasonal fruit. For drinks, she'd recommend a bottle of Txakoli and her home-made *aguas frescas*.

As she spelled out her plans, Everly nodded her agreement and Claire relaxed with each minute that went by. While she was confident in her ability to cook, satisfying a crowd of people accustomed to the best was daunting. Plus, what she might have fixed for a San Francisco crowd wouldn't necessarily cut it in Charleston.

"Another thought would be to offer wines made by someone who plays polo." Claire went on to list a couple brands that she'd researched.

"Well, aren't you thorough," Everly said, looking surprised.

The waitress brought their food, interrupting the flow of the conversation, and Claire picked up her fork, eager to taste what she'd chosen. Magnolias was known for their refined take on Southern cuisine. The menu had offered several dishes featuring fried green tomatoes, creamy grits and, of course, shellfish. But one dish in particular had caught her eye: a bourbon fried catfish with pickled hot peppers, okra and sweet corn fricassee, and Tabasco rémoulade.

Everly ignored her own plate of delicious-looking scallops. "After Bettina's party, I knew that you were a fantastic chef, but your suggestions today are so much better than I expected. What made you think of the wine made by polo players?"

"I remember reading an article about the Argentinian wineries building polo fields because the pairing made so much sense."

"It's brilliant. Have you ever considered opening

your own catering company? Someone with your talent could be a big hit in Charleston. I have a lot of connections in town and could help you get started."

"That's really nice of you," Claire said, appreciating Everly's enthusiasm but wishing everyone would stop trying to push her into something she wasn't ready for. "But I'm not interested in catering full-time."

"I don't see why not. I recognize talent when I see it."

"Thank you, but I like working for Linc and don't intend to stop."

"But your talent is wasted." At last, Everly picked up her fork and turned her attention to her meal. "You could be doing so much more than just cleaning Linc Thurston's house."

"To be honest, I don't know where to begin when it comes to launching a business. I'm only catering these few events because Bettina is Linc's mother and your committee members seemed in a desperate situation."

"I understand that starting a business must seem daunting. But here's how I can help you. I belong to an organization of women entrepreneurs and we make it our mission to support and encourage people like you."

"That sounds like a worthwhile mission," Claire said, "but I don't have the time or money to start my own catering company." *Why wouldn't this woman stop pushing?*

"I understand your concerns, but I'm sure you can work something out. You don't have to do it all at once. Why don't we get together after the polo match and I can walk you through some of the options. Your food is so good. I just know you'd be a huge success."

Sensing the woman wouldn't drop it, Claire managed a vague smile and a half-hearted nod. This encounter with Everly reinforced for Claire why she had no interest in starting a catering business. Too often, she struggled to assert herself. As a kid, she'd never learned to stand and fight. It was always easier to run away.

Fortunately for Claire, as the two women ate, she was able to turn the tables on Everly and persuade her to talk about her own background. Claire wasn't surprised that, although Everly spoke about growing up in Charleston, she never mentioned her sister who'd been imprisoned for stealing.

When lunch was over, Everly snagged the check as soon as the waitress set it down and slid her credit card into the holder, ignoring Claire's protest.

"My treat," the blonde said. "You are saving us from a disaster. The least I could do is buy you lunch. Besides, I suggested eating here and I know it's a little expensive."

"Thank you," Claire replied, deciding against letting the subtle jab get to her.

Still, no matter how much Everly complimented her talents as a chef, the Charlestonian would always view Claire as "the help." It was this prejudicial view that Linc couldn't seem to understand or refused to acknowledge despite growing up in this town.

No matter how successful or rich she became, as far as everyone who mattered was concerned, Claire would never be good enough for Linc. Although it put an ache in her heart, she'd accepted it. If only he would as well.

Because if he didn't, his faith in them as a couple was going to tear them apart sooner rather than later.

Claire stood beside Linc and marveled as the mass of horses and riders charged from one end of the field to the other in pursuit of a small white ball. The thunder of the hooves on the grass made her heart pound. She hadn't been prepared for the adrenaline rush of watching the nonstop action of a polo match.

It was the second match of the day. She'd been occupied getting the luncheon baskets ready and missed the first. For some reason, she'd assumed polo was like other sports where it would take hours to play the game. Today, she'd discovered that the match was composed of six chukkers—or periods—lasting seven and a half minutes each, with a ten-minute halftime during which the spectators went out onto the field for the traditional divot stomp.

"What do you think?" Linc asked.

Flushed with enthusiasm, she glanced away from the field, noting that several of the ladies dressed in party frocks with adorable hats festooned with ribbons and flowers were paying more attention to her and Linc than the match.

"The spectators appear so civilized," she said, grinning up at him. "While the polo riders are intense and a little crazy."

The sport wasn't for the fainthearted. Four horses from each team galloped down the field, bumping and jockeying for position while their riders swung four-foot mallets. It was a wonder no one was seriously hurt.

A cry went up from the crowd as Sawyer's friend Ruby scored yet again for the women. This particular match was a battle of the sexes, and at the moment, the women were kicking butt.

"How come you don't play?" Claire asked Linc. She'd noticed that several of his friends were on teams today.

Linc shook his head. "I like to keep both my feet on the ground when I'm chasing little white balls."

"Have you tried it?"

"Once. It didn't go well." Linc's grin was rueful. "Do you ride? I'm sure Ruby would be happy to give you some lessons in how to play."

Although Claire had never been on a horse, she could imagine how empowering it would feel to charge down the field in pursuit of the ball at speeds of thirty to forty miles an hour. "I don't think so."

"Why not?"

"It must take years to learn to ride well enough to do this."

"You wouldn't play at this level to start off. I'm sure there are plenty of people who are beginners that you could team up with."

Though intrigued, Claire shook her head. She didn't have the time or the money to spend on something like polo.

"Linc, there you are." It was Landry Beaumont, yet another stunning woman with her sights set on Linc. "Where did you disappear to after lunch? It's nearly halftime. Come meet my brother. He's on Austin's team. We can harass them about losing to a bunch of girls."

While Linc was distracted by Landry, Claire faded from his side, fighting the dismay swelling in her chest. What had she expected? She'd known from the first that anything between her and Linc was temporary at best.

And from what she'd gleaned after Bettina's party, it sounded like everyone was rooting for a relationship to develop between Linc and Landry. With her family connections, beauty and interests, she was being touted as the perfect girl for him.

Done with her work, Claire headed for the exit, her foolish heart aching. Unfortunately, her escape was thwarted by Everly Briggs.

"There you are," Everly said. Today, she wore a filmy floral dress in various warm pastel shades, a broad-brimmed hat festooned with poppies, and dark glasses. "You're not leaving already, are you?"

Feeling shabby beside the socialite, Claire nodded. "It's been a long day and I should be getting back to my daughter."

"Well, then, I'm so glad I caught you. You did a terrific job for us today. Do you have all the receipts so I can get our treasurer to write a check for you?"

The last thing Claire wanted was to be delayed, but she'd paid for the food out of her own pocket and needed to be reimbursed. "I have everything in my car."

"Can you get it and bring it back here? I'll go find Deirdre."

"Of course."

Claire made her way through the parking lot to her Saab and retrieved the folder that held all her receipts, as well as the paperwork the committee had requested she fill out so they could reimburse her.

When she arrived at the spot where she and Everly had parted, the other woman hadn't yet returned. While she waited, Claire's gaze roved the crowd in search of Linc's tall form. She spotted him with Austin and a blond man she assumed was Landry's brother, since the group also included her and Ruby.

"Well, look who's here," said a familiar female voice from just behind her shoulder.

Claire's head snapped around and there stood Jasper's mother and father. The malicious satisfaction in their expressions caused Claire to step back from them.

"Doug. Sharon." Claire couldn't believe what she was seeing. "What are you doing here?"

"You look surprised." Doug Patmore sneered. "Didn't think we would find you?"

Of average height with tanned skin and a fleshy face, Jasper's father used the force of his personality rather than his physical presence to intimidate. Claire had never cared for the way he invaded her space. She suspected he enjoyed her discomfort.

The incongruity of seeing these two in Charleston, at a polo match, a party she was catering, left her dumbfounded and mute.

"Where's our granddaughter?" Sharon demanded. "You had no right to take her away from us and we insist on seeing her at once to make sure she's okay."

The accusation made Claire want to shriek. Their outrageous claims were the reason why she'd packed up and fled California not long after Jasper's death.

She was terrified she might lose Honey once his parents started challenging her for custody of their granddaughter.

Logically, she knew that they might not have enough against her to convince a judge that Honey wasn't safe in her care, but she wasn't confident that the system would work for her this time after it had failed her seven years earlier when a lie had branded Claire as dangerous to children.

And with Jasper dead, who would believe his parents were poor guardians? It would be her word against both of theirs if she claimed that as soon as he graduated high school, Jasper had gone into the military and cut all ties with his parents.

"Honey is perfectly fine." It was an effort to keep her voice calm and steady when her whole body trembled with fear and fury. "And I haven't changed my mind about you seeing her."

Their distress at being kept from their granddaughter spun Claire's emotions into a chaotic mess. On one hand, Jasper was their only son, and even though they'd driven him away over fifteen years earlier, Claire recognized that they might want to try to do better with his daughter.

Unfortunately, they'd shown themselves to be toxic people and had resisted Claire's attempts to deal fairly with them. From the moment they reached out to her after Jasper's death, they hadn't had a single nice thing to say and had even gone so far as to accuse her of deliberately getting pregnant to force Jasper to take care of her.

"You will let us see her now," Jasper's father stated, his voice rising. "Or we will call the authorities."

Although Claire never took her eyes off the pair, she became aware that heads were turning in their direction. The last thing she needed was for the stir to reach Linc. He'd feel compelled to come see if she was okay. Then he'd meet Jasper's parents and find out that she'd been lying to him for over a year.

"Honey is our granddaughter," Sharon said, picking up the argument. "We need to make sure she's safe. You had no right to take her away from us."

Claire ground her teeth. She had every right to move across the country and away from these people. Jasper had told her numerous stories of his childhood and how he'd been verbally abused if he got a couple answers wrong on a test or didn't get his chores done fast enough. She couldn't imagine entrusting her sweet-natured baby to these unhappy, abrasive people.

Claire tried again. "Let's go somewhere and talk. We don't want to disturb this lovely function."

"I don't give a damn about this party," Jasper's mother said. "I just want my grandbaby."

"Is everything okay?" To Claire's dismay, Linc was approaching with Knox and Sawyer trailing after him.

"Everything is fine," she answered.

"Everything is not fine," Jasper's mother declared. "This girl has stolen our granddaughter from us."

"That's not true," Claire said. She couldn't look at Linc. This sort of outrageous scene was the height of disrespect. What he must think of her.

"Are you Claire's family?" he asked, his deep voice

ringing with authority and bringing a much-needed calm to the situation.

"Her family?" Doug Patmore gave a caustic laugh. "Hardly. She wanted to marry our son, but we wouldn't have her."

That wasn't true. At least the part about her wanting to marry Jasper. No doubt Jasper's parents blamed her for their estrangement from their son, even though it had begun years before she and Jasper had ever met.

Linc was frowning at Jasper's parents. "I'm sorry, but I'm confused. Claire was married to your son."

"Well, that's a pack of lies," Jasper's father said, his eyes narrowing as he regarded Claire. "I guess we shouldn't be surprised, considering the way you duped my son into thinking you gave a damn about him and got pregnant so he'd have to take care of you."

Horror kept Claire pinned in place even as the desire to crawl under a shrub and die flooded her. She told herself not to glance Linc's way for his reaction, but she simply had to know if he believed the lies Jasper's father was spouting.

Linc's face was an impenetrable mask. Only his eyes expressed the deep sadness and crushing disappointment he was feeling.

"You were never married?" he asked her, his voice low and husky.

Her gaze flickered to Jasper's parents. It was all over. She might as well come clean. There'd been no future for her and Linc anyway. But watching his faith in her crumble was a blow she hadn't seen coming.

"No."

Ten

Scarcely able to believe that Claire had been lying to him this whole time, Linc tried to get his head around what was going on. She wasn't a military widow, or any sort of widow. Had any of what she'd said been true? Or had she simply been playing him all along?

"Why did you tell everyone you were?" he demanded.

Instead of rushing into an explanation of her actions, she crossed her arms over her chest and glanced at the older couple who'd been harassing her as he walked up.

She ducked her head and spoke in a low voice. "Can we please talk about this later?"

"Why can't you just tell me?" Linc growled, staring at the woman he'd started thinking in terms of spending the rest of his life with, willing her to say something—

anything—that would make the churning in his gut go away. "Claire, what the hell is going on? Who are these people?"

"Jasper's parents. Doug and Sharon Patmore."

"What are they doing here?"

Claire shook her head. "Can we please talk about this later?"

Knox set his hand on Linc's arm. "The media is going to be all over this if we don't step away right now."

A portion of his mind registered that Sawyer was also standing beside him. Their support meant everything in that moment. Unfortunately, they weren't the only ones there. Linc glanced around, noticing several people clicking away on their phones. The curiosity of the crowd surrounding them was palpable. No doubt, dozens of social media posts were being uploaded that very second.

"Knox is right," Claire said, her eyes wide and pleading. "You don't want to get dragged into any sort of a scene."

And before he could say another word, she darted away, headed in the opposite direction from the older couple she'd been speaking with. They started off after her and Linc's gut twisted as he watched them all disappear into the crowd. Letting her go taxed his willpower.

Despite knowing she'd lied, his instincts told him to follow and fight at her side. It was pretty obvious that the older couple were up to no good. He'd never seen Claire look so miserable.

"Any idea what that was about?" Knox asked. "They accused Claire of stealing their granddaughter."

"That's ridiculous." Linc might not know Claire as well as he'd assumed, but he doubted she'd do anything like that. "There's something strange going on here and I'd like to get to the bottom of it."

"So you didn't know she was never married?"

Linc shook his head. "She's been lying to all of us."

"Why would she do that?" Sawyer murmured, sliding her hand around his arm and giving a gentle squeeze.

Linc glanced at Sawyer and nodded his appreciation of her comforting gesture. "I don't know, but there's something wrong with those people claiming to be Honey's grandparents. Claire once told me her... Jasper didn't have any sort of relationship with his parents and didn't want them near Honey. If that's the case, I wonder what they're doing here."

"Claire sure didn't look happy to see them," Sawyer added.

He knew better than to feel sympathy for Claire, but he couldn't help it.

"So if she didn't invite them, how did they know to find her here?" Knox asked.

"That's a good question," Linc said. "Maybe we need to find out how they got in."

"I can check with Portia and see if they were on the list of people who bought tickets," Knox offered.

When Linc nodded, Knox headed off, leaving brother and sister by themselves.

"Are you going to be okay?" Sawyer asked.

"I'm perfectly fine," Linc said. "Just surprised, that's all."

But from his sister's expression, Linc realized he'd

given away that he felt more for Claire than what a boss feels for an employee. And if he didn't take himself in hand right now, the entire world would know he'd been behaving like a complete idiot.

"Are you and Claire…" Sawyer paused and glanced around, but they were out of earshot. "Have you been sleeping together?"

"Only just recently."

"Linc." She packed a world of concern into the single syllable.

"You don't need to tell me I screwed up."

And yet, until a moment ago, he'd been convinced that he'd had it all figured out. When he imagined the rest of his life, he pictured every day with Claire and Honey in it. Not as his housekeeper, but as something more permanent. Wife. The word didn't trigger any sort of alarm. It should have. Given what he'd learned just now.

The kicker was he still wanted her in his life. Knowing she'd lied to him and that he had no true idea of who she was, he still couldn't imagine anyone who made him as happy as she did.

"I don't think you screwed up," Sawyer said.

Hadn't he? Linc reminded himself he'd done all the pursuing. If he hadn't let his feelings for her be known, would she have slept with him? In fact, she'd resisted all his attempts to move their relationship forward. But if he took her at her word and believed she never intended their relationship to be public, then why had she created a fictitious husband?

"We need to get more information before we judge

her," Sawyer continued. "Claire isn't malicious and I can't imagine her setting out to hurt you. In fact, when she was talking to those people, I thought she looked afraid."

He nodded. "I thought so, too." And suddenly, he couldn't believe he'd let worry about bad publicity keep him from helping her. "I have to go find her and figure out what's going on."

Claire picked up speed as she broke away from Jasper's parents and Linc. Uppermost in her mind was escaping the polo grounds and getting to her daughter. The decisions she needed to make could wait until she held Honey in her arms once more.

"Claire!" Everly Briggs was bearing down on her. "Where are you going? I thought we were going to meet up so I could get you the money we owe you."

"I have the receipts here. Can you mail me the check? I need to leave."

As she extended the folder to Everly, Claire glanced over her shoulder, looking for the Patmores. But she didn't see Jasper's parents. Maybe she'd given them the slip. She sure hoped so. The thought of them following her to Linc's house alarmed her.

"Is something wrong?" Everly made no attempt to take the folder from Claire. "You seem upset. Has something happened?"

"My address is on the paperwork." She'd secured a PO Box when she'd first arrived in Charleston and had all her mail sent there.

"Did you and Linc have a fight?"

"What?"

"I saw him a few seconds ago and noticed that he looked angry. Did you fight about how much time he spent with Landry Beaumont today?" Everly's green eyes gleamed with interest. "Jealousy doesn't suit you."

Claire stared at the woman in dumbfounded silence. "I'm not jealous."

"Because you think he's going to pick you over her?" Everly laughed, and it wasn't a nice sound. "That's never going to happen. You're not in her league."

"You don't think I know that?"

It was hard always being treated like she wasn't good enough. First, her mother had walked out on Claire. Then her father chose his new family over her. Maybe there was something wrong with her, because she'd become embroiled in a relationship with Linc knowing she was even less suitable than his former fiancée.

"And it doesn't matter," Claire continued. "Linc and I aren't involved."

"Who do you think you're kidding?" Everly leaned in and pinned Claire with a malicious stare. "I watched the two of you together and saw exactly what's going on. You're sleeping with him."

Claire recoiled, wondering how such a fun day had gone to hell so fast. She was opening her mouth to deny Everly's claim when they were interrupted by a familiar voice.

"There you are," Jasper's mother said. "Don't think you can get away so easily."

"Who are these people?" Everly demanded, assessing the Patmores with a frown. "Did you invite them?"

"No."

"How did you get in here?" Everly continued.

"Not that it's any of your business," Doug Patmore said, "but we had tickets."

Seeing this answer wasn't going to satisfy Everly, Claire decided the sooner she got Jasper's parents out of there, the better. Rather than argue with them any further near witnesses, Claire once again broke off and headed in the direction of the parking lot. As she expected, the Patmores were hot on her heels.

"Where do you think you're going?" Doug demanded, panting a little as he caught up with her.

"Away from you." But as they reached the parking lot, Claire slowed down so she could ask the question uppermost in her thoughts. "How did you find me in Charleston and how did you know where I would be today?"

"A woman called us and said you'd moved here," Sharon said.

Doug nodded. "She said you'd taken up with some ballplayer and were living with him."

"What woman?" Claire demanded, gripping her car keys as her blood ran cold. Who would go to all the trouble to do something like that?

"She didn't give us her name, but she said she was from Charleston and had met you at a party." Jasper's father looked disgusted. "Is that what you've been doing since you've been here? Neglecting our granddaughter while you go out carousing at night?"

"The only party I've attended was one I catered recently. I was working, not carousing."

Claire thought back to Bettina's party. Was it possible that one of the guests had suspected something was going on between her and Linc and decided that she needed to be out of the picture? That was crazy. No one in their right mind would consider Claire competition. But what other explanation could there be? And how would anyone have known how to find Jasper's parents? She hadn't told anyone his last name. Would someone have gone so far as to have her investigated? If so, it was a despicable thing to do.

"What about the baseball player you're shacked up with?" Doug asked. "Is he doing drugs and partying? What sort of environment is that for our granddaughter?"

If she wasn't used to their harassment, these sorts of accusations might've shocked Claire. But it wasn't much different from what they'd thrown at her in San Francisco and reinforced why she'd left. Even though she'd told herself that it was difficult for grandparents to take custody of a child away from its mother, she didn't trust that the system always worked the way it was supposed to. Nor did she have the means to fight a lengthy battle against Jasper's parents.

"He doesn't party," Claire said. "And where I'm living is none of your business."

"I'll bet he has money," Jasper's father said, his eyes narrowing to slits.

She shook her head. "What does that have to do with anything?"

"Maybe you don't want to lose your meal ticket."

"My meal ticket?" Until Jasper's death, Claire hadn't

had any contact with his parents and everything since then had been negative, but this was beyond anything she'd expected. "What are you talking about?"

"Seems to us that you have a sweet situation here."

What was he trying to get at? Claire looked from Doug to Sharon and back again. The disgust on their faces set something off. Shame flooded her. She wasn't the horrible person they imagined, but there was no question that she'd been sleeping with Linc and behaving recklessly.

"Give us our sweet baby," Sharon said, "and we'll leave you be."

"She's not your sweet baby." Fury burned away Claire's confusion. The idea of running again filled her with dread, but the last thing she was going to do was let Jasper's parents take her daughter. "Jasper didn't want you in his life and he certainly didn't want you in his daughter's life, either."

"Better us than you. We're going to get her one way or another."

Claire shook her head and tried to look confident, even as she cringed inside. "You have no grounds to take Honey away from me."

"I'm sure there is a judge in California that would disagree with you."

"But we're not in California." It was all a huge bluff on her part. Claire wasn't sure if what had happened when she was twenty would have any bearing on a court case here in South Carolina.

"You might think you're safe here, but we could

make things pretty uncomfortable for you," Jasper's mother said.

"You and that Linc Thurston fellow," Doug Patmore agreed.

When Jasper's dad spoke Linc's name, Claire went cold all over. The last thing she wanted to do was drag Linc into a scandal, and it looked like Jasper's father was eager to make trouble.

"I'm not going to give you my daughter," Claire growled, feeling very much like a cornered mama bear. The more time she spent with Jasper's parents, the more convinced she became that she would do whatever it took to keep Honey away from them.

"Then give us the hundred thousand dollars she got."

"What hundred thousand dollars?"

"Don't play dumb with us. She's the beneficiary of his death benefit for being killed in active duty. That's a hundred thousand tax-free."

With those words, the whole reason for their interest in their granddaughter became crystal clear. As Honey's guardians, they would be able to control that death benefit. A hundred thousand dollars was a lot of money.

"I don't have it." In truth, it had never occurred to her that there might be something Honey would receive after Jasper's death.

"You are a terrible liar," Doug said. "Of course you have it."

Claire shook her head. "I never applied for any money."

"Well, then, you're an even bigger idiot than we

thought." Doug exchanged a look with his wife. "You need to get us that money."

"But it belongs to Honey." A second earlier, Claire had been willing to do whatever it took to protect her daughter. That money would go a long way toward securing Honey's future. "And I know Jasper would want her to have it."

"He's our son. We raised him. If anyone should get the money, it's us, not some mistake he made with you."

Claire sucked in a deep breath to bolster her courage and set her chin at a defiant angle. For her daughter's sake, she would not let these people bully her.

"You're wasting your breath," Claire said, no longer afraid that they could take Honey from her now that she had their measure. "You aren't getting my daughter and you aren't getting any money. Go back to San Francisco and leave us alone."

And with that, Claire turned her back on Jasper's parents and strode away. But she wasn't moving fast enough to escape Doug Patmore's final words.

"Give us that money or we'll make sure everyone knows what you've been up to with your boss. You might not care what people say about you, but I'll bet he and that family of his will."

Eleven

Even though Linc knew he should stay at the charity event until all the polo matches were done, he couldn't focus on anything but the expression on Claire's face when she'd admitted that she'd been lying to him for a year. As it was, he stuck around long enough only for Knox to report that no one by the name of Patmore had bought tickets to the event.

But someone had gotten tickets for them. Someone who'd hoped Jasper's parents would make a scene at a public event to embarrass Claire. But why? Linc knew he couldn't wait much longer to find out.

To his relief, Claire's car was parked in the driveway when he arrived home. But upon entering the house, Linc spied two suitcases sitting in the kitchen near the back door and stopped dead while his brain tried to wrap itself around the reason they were there.

Claire was leaving him.

Just as he arrived at that conclusion, she entered the kitchen carrying Honey. As soon as the toddler spied him, she lifted both her arms, opening and closing her fists in a double wave that put a lump in his throat. It hit him then that no matter what Claire had done or how angry he was with her, he couldn't bear to let her go.

"Where are you going?" he demanded, more pain than accusation in his voice.

She gazed at him in wide-eyed dismay. "Why are you here? You're supposed to be at the polo match."

"I left early because I needed to talk to you." He gestured at the luggage. "Are you running out on me?"

Before she could answer, he plucked Honey from her arms. The toddler cooed with delight and wrapped her arms around his neck. She smelled faintly of her mother's perfume mixed with baby lotion. He breathed in the familiar scent, relieved that he'd been in time to stop these two from vanishing from his life.

"I'm not running out on you. I'm leaving before I embroil you in a huge scandal."

"As if I care what people say about me," he said, keeping his tone calm, not wanting to upset Honey.

"You should. Your family and friends do."

"Are you ready to tell me what the hell is going on?" He asked the question without any heat, just needing to understand. "Why did you tell everyone you were married?"

Claire stared at the floor without answering for so

long he wasn't sure if she would speak without further prodding. But then after a long-suffering sigh, she walked to the sunroom and pulled out Honey's toys.

"Bring her in here. She can play while we talk."

Once Honey was occupied with a sorting game, Claire went into the kitchen and began emptying the dishwasher. The mundane task seemed to soothe her, and as she put plates and cups away, she began to explain.

"I discovered when I first moved to Charleston that being a military widow with a child made people more likely to give me a chance. Was it wrong?" She nodded emphatically. "Absolutely. But I don't think I'd change what I did."

"But why didn't you come clean with me? I wouldn't have judged you."

"I wanted to." Claire didn't meet his eyes. "I should have."

"I don't understand what stopped you."

"At first, it was because I needed the job as your housekeeper. Living here meant I could stay under the radar. Jasper's parents would have a harder time finding me."

"Why were you trying to avoid them?"

"Before Jasper went overseas the last time, he made me promise that I would keep our child away from his parents. Their relationship was strained and he was afraid they would treat his child the way they behaved toward him."

"But you're her mother, and you don't have to give them access to her."

"They made things very uncomfortable for me. Plus…"

She looked incredibly uncomfortable. What was she so reluctant to say? He couldn't reconcile the woman he had come to care for this past year with this secretive individual who'd spun one lie after another.

"At the party, they said you'd stolen their granddaughter. What aren't you telling me?"

"They were the reason I left California."

"You moved all the way across the country to keep Honey away from her grandparents?"

Claire nodded. "They threatened to take her away from me."

"You're her mother," Linc said. "There's no way that could happen."

"Unfortunately, if they decided to push the issue, there was a possibility that I could've been deemed an unfit mother and lost her."

"An unfit mother?" *Was this another lie?* It seemed impossible that she could believe something so far-fetched. "You're the furthest thing from it."

"There was an incident back when I'd just turned twenty." Her eyes darted in his direction and then away. She was obviously grappling with something. "I told you my father got remarried. It was pretty obvious from the start that Aubrey wanted my father to focus on her and their new family, and she got it into her head that I resented her."

"Did you?" Linc recalled Claire telling him that her stepmother was only eight years older than her. "It seemed like your dad was all the family you had for most of your life."

"I will admit that at sixteen I wasn't thrilled when Aubrey moved in. She and my dad had been dating for about six months and she'd gotten pregnant. I never knew if they got married because he loved her or if he just felt responsible for the baby. Either way, once she came to live with us, everything changed. She had really strong opinions about everything and wasn't shy about asserting herself."

Linc recalled how Sawyer had been at sixteen and remembered epic battles with their mother over nothing. It wasn't hard to imagine Claire and her stepmother locked in a power struggle. After all, Claire had been the only woman in her father's life for nine years after her mother had left. No doubt, she'd taken care of him as much as she'd been taken care of. Giving that up couldn't have been easy.

"I understand, but what does this have to do with your concern that Honey's grandparents could interfere with your custody of her?"

"By the time I turned twenty, Aubrey had given birth to my half brother, Shane, and half sister, Grace. Shane was a total momma's boy and a terror. I moved out right after high school because of how bad things were between Aubrey and me. She made sure I wasn't welcome and I stopped visiting."

Linc remembered how it had hurt when his father had left them after serving his five-year sentence. The betrayal Linc had felt after he, Sawyer and their mother had stuck by him during the trial and scandal, and made regular trips to visit him in prison.

At least he'd had his sister and mother. Who had supported Claire?

She lied to you.

While it was important to remind himself of that fact, Linc was starting to soften his stance toward Claire. Especially when what she'd done hadn't actively hurt anyone. Could he really blame her for doing whatever it took to survive?

"My dad didn't understand what was going on between us," Claire continued, "and I knew it hurt him that I never came around anymore. So, on Grace's second birthday, I went to her party. Shane was acting out worse than usual because his sister was getting all the attention."

Linc had little trouble picturing the scene. Claire's discomfort as she recounted the story was palpable. Obviously, whatever had happened continued to bother her.

"When it was time for cake and opening presents, Shane was nowhere to be found. Aubrey was making a big deal out of wanting him to be there when Grace blew out her candles, so I went to find him. He'd gone up into this little tree house my dad had built for him."

With each sentence, Claire tensed. Her fingers tightened and straightened. Linc's gut became a solid knot of discomfort as he suspected where the tale might lead.

"Was it high?"

"Not more than six feet off the ground, but high enough that a child falling out of it could get hurt."

"And is that what happened?"

Claire nodded. She let loose a shaky breath and kept going. "I started out at the bottom, trying to coax him to come down, but he didn't like me very much. I think he'd picked up on the antagonism between his mother and me. Anyway, I ended up climbing up into the tree house, hoping to talk some sense into him. But he started screaming at me and told me to go away, acting like I was scaring him half to death." A mirthless smile twisted her lips. "The little brat was good at making scenes and knew exactly how to manipulate his mother. Anyway, I was on the verge of leaving him be when he decided to go out the window and try to climb across to a nearby branch."

"Did he make it?"

"Yes, but once he got there, he lost his balance. I tried to grab him, but he was just out of reach and he fell." Claire closed her eyes for a long second. "Because he was making such a fuss, a bunch of the guests were looking our way, and from their angle, they said it looked like I'd pushed him."

"You can't be serious."

Even before she answered, Claire's grim expression told him just how bad things had been. "Needless to say, Aubrey's family already disliked me and I think one of them called child protective services, claiming I was a danger to the kids."

"Surely no one could possibly have believed that."

"Those sorts of agencies get things wrong all the time. It didn't help that Shane also claimed I'd pushed him. He ended up with a broken arm and devoured all the attention he got that day." As the story wound down, Claire trailed off with a sigh.

Linc remembered how he'd encouraged her to take some time off and go home to visit her family. He understood now why she hadn't looked all that excited about it.

"When the findings came back from the social worker that I posed a potential danger to my half siblings, I realized that maintaining a relationship with my father was going to be tough."

"I can't believe your father believed you could hurt them. What is your relationship with him like now?"

"I think he feels bad, but he's married to Aubrey and has a responsibility to their children. We talk when she's not around and he came to visit me in the hospital after Honey was born. When I told him what Jasper's parents were trying to do, he gave me some money to help me get out of San Francisco and start over somewhere new. I know he'd like to do more, but..." She trailed off.

Linc ached, seeing her pain. "That's not fair to you."

"And it's made me wary of trusting people." She cast a burning look his way from beneath her lashes. "Even those I want to."

He caught her meaning and gave a small nod. "So this business with Shane and child protective services stepping in is what Jasper's parents have against you?"

"Yes. I'm not sure how they found out about it, but when they started threatening me for custody of Honey, I left town."

"You could've fought it. All you needed was a good lawyer."

"I couldn't afford one. With the high cost of living in

California, it was all I could do to keep my head above water. And I was too afraid if I'd stayed to fight them that I might lose Honey." Tears glinted at the corners of her eyes. "I bought a car and a friend of mine registered it in his name. Then I drove across country, stopping in small towns and picking up odd jobs here and there. It took me nearly six months to get to Charleston. I wasn't sure how long I was going to stick around, but then I met your mother and she thought I'd be a good fit for your housekeeper. It's been great working for you and living here. It's the first time since learning Jasper was dead that I've felt safe. I should've known it wouldn't last."

"How did the Patmores find you?"

"I don't have a clue. I've been careful to stay under the radar. I suppose they could've hired someone. But even if they'd located me in Charleston, to show up at the party like that is so odd. Because there was no doubt they were there specifically to find me."

"Someone in Charleston must have tipped them off," Linc said thoughtfully. "But for what purpose?"

Claire's brown eyes looked huge in her pale face. "Because they figured out we're involved and want me out of the picture."

"What? Don't be ridiculous."

"Jasper's parents knew all about you and threatened to go public with a bunch of lies unless I paid them off."

"How much do they want?"

"A hundred thousand dollars. It's the amount Honey would receive from the military because her father died in the line of duty." Claire's chin went up and her eyes grew cold. "But I'm not going to pay it to them."

"Of course not." But Linc would have no qualms about parting with the sum if it gave Claire some peace of mind. He was busy calculating the wisdom of paying off blackmailers when Claire made her stunning announcement.

"Honey and I are going to leave Charleston instead."

Linc was shaking his head before Claire finished speaking. "Absolutely not. You've lost your mind if you think I'm going to let you leave Charleston." From the tone of his voice, he meant every word. "Whatever it takes to keep you here is what we'll do."

"But this isn't your problem," she protested. "It's mine, and I refuse to let you be dragged into my mess."

"But it's not your mess. You didn't cause the problem. Vile people are trying to take advantage of you. Let me help you stop them."

"Don't you understand?" Her heart hammered in her chest at the fierce determination on his face. "This isn't your fight."

As much as she longed to surrender to his will and accept his protection, her doubts were stronger. No one had ever had her back before. She also couldn't forget his anger at the polo grounds.

"I'm making it my fight."

"But the scandal…"

"There won't be any scandal—" he grasped her chin and brought her gaze to his "—if you marry me."

"What?" She jerked free and took a half step back,

her senses reeling as if he'd slapped her. "Your mother will never accept me. London was beautiful, wealthy and sophisticated and she wasn't good enough. I'll always be the woman who cleaned your house. Think of how it will look. I can't do that to you."

"My mother knows how I feel about you. All she wants is for me to be happy."

Claire covered her eyes with her hands, blocking out his earnest expression. Immediately, her other senses took over. She inhaled his familiar cologne and listened to the rough cadence of his breathing.

"You were happy with London," she reminded him, "and that didn't improve Bettina's opinion of her."

"I never should've proposed to London." Linc tugged her hands down so he could meet her gaze. "She wasn't the love of my life. You are."

Her chest tightened at his words. "We haven't known each other long enough for you to believe that." What would it take for him to realize this was crazy? How could he possibly love her? She'd made so many mistakes. "And I lied to you."

"All that is true, but it doesn't change that I love you."

Claire hunched her shoulders. With her head and her heart locked in a fierce battle, all she could do was keep trying to make him see reason.

"It won't work," she said. "You'll see."

"It can and it will. All you need to do is trust me."

She shook her head. "I do trust you, but there are greater forces at work in your life than how we feel about each other."

"How do we feel about each other?" he asked, taking

her by the shoulders. The pressure of his warm fingers brought her close to tears. "I love you. I want to marry you and for us to be a family."

"Damn it, Linc. Be reasonable."

He ignored her objection. "How do you feel about me?"

A sob bloomed in her chest, making her breath erratic. While the words she'd longed to speak stuck in her throat, Claire grappled with fear. If she opened her heart and told him the truth—that she couldn't bear the thought of living without him—he would never let her go. And then what if all his friends and family opposed their relationship? How could she hope to make Linc happy?

"I love you," she confessed, her strong emotions refusing to remain bottled up any longer.

"That's my girl." He cupped her face in his palms and leaned down to graze her lips with his. "It feels like I've been waiting forever to hear those words from you."

"But, Linc, we can't—"

He stopped her words with another kiss, this one longer and deeper. She was light-headed and giddy by the time he lifted his head.

"Let's just focus on you, me and Honey. No one else matters."

"But they do. Maybe in a thousand other cities things would be different. But in Charleston, everyone's opinion matters."

"So we'll live in Texas or California or wherever you want. What matters is that we're together."

She couldn't believe what he was saying. "But your

family and friends are here. And say what you want, but the fact is they are important to you."

"So what will it take?"

"For what?"

"For you to marry me in a huge ceremony in front of all our friends and family? I want to shout my love for you from the rooftops."

His question overwhelmed her, but she recognized that running was impossible now. Even if it was the smartest thing for everyone, hope had seized control. What if she and Linc could make a go of things? She loved him. Could she really turn her back on a chance for happiness?

"I can't honestly say what would change my mind," she said, but in fact, she knew. If by some miracle the family origin legend was true and she was descended from an old Charleston family...

"You underestimate how persuasive I can be." A wicked grin lit up his expression.

"Well, there's a welcome sight."

Claire glanced toward the back door and spied Sawyer standing just inside the kitchen.

"What are you doing here?" Linc demanded.

"Interrupting something, obviously." Wearing an unrepentant grin, Sawyer strode toward them and snagged Claire by the arm, tugging her away from Linc. "Excuse us, brother dear. I need to speak with Claire."

"What's going on?"

"Give Mom a call. She wants to know if you're interested in coming by for dinner. Claire and I will be right back."

Claire bit her lip as Sawyer led her toward the front of the house. Her stomach, still unsettled by the day's events, began churning in earnest as Sawyer directed her into the living room and onto the tufted cobalt sofa.

"What's going on?" she asked, echoing Linc's earlier question. "Did something happen after I left the polo event today? Does everyone know what's been going on between Linc and me? Is that why your mother wants him to come over for dinner? So she can tell him to send me packing?"

And yet, wasn't that what she'd been all ready to do mere minutes earlier? To disappear out of Linc's life? What was so different now that he'd told her he loved her and wanted to marry her?

"Nothing like that," Sawyer assured her. "As for Mother, she's delighted that Linc has found someone who makes him as happy as you do."

"She knows about me? About us? How did she find out?" Claire sagged back against the sofa and closed her eyes. "I'm so embarrassed."

"Linc told her the day after the party. I don't think he went into any great detail about what you two have been up to, but she knows he loves you."

Claire sat up and stared at Sawyer. "Then what is it you needed to tell me?"

"What I found out from my friend at the historical society about your ancestor James Robbins."

"What you found out?" Claire regarded Sawyer in confusion. "I don't understand. How did you know about him?"

"Linc told me your story, so I went to the historical society and did some digging to find out about the Robbins family."

Claire couldn't believe Sawyer's excitement over what she'd found and noticed her own pulse picking up speed. Although her great-aunt had believed the stories of James Robbins leaving behind his Charleston family to chase his fortune in the California gold rush, part of Claire hadn't quite believed that there was anything more to the tales than family legend.

"So there's a Robbins family in Charleston?"

Sawyer shook her head. "Not anymore. They died out when their first son was killed during the Civil War."

"Oh." Claire struggled to contain her rising disappointment. What a fool she was to think maybe she had a connection to a family that might impress Bettina. "Well, thanks for looking."

"Not so fast. Just because the Robbins name died out doesn't mean they weren't an important Charleston family. There was a daughter. Penelope. She married well and had lots of descendants."

It hadn't occurred to Claire that after all this time she might actually have family living in Charleston. She'd been focused on the members of her great-great-grandfather's generation and determining if James Robbins had been telling the truth. "What would they be? My distant cousins?"

"It will take a while to sort out all the genealogies and how everyone connects to you, but I know for sure that you're related to the Haskells. As in my friend Shelby Haskell." Sawyer beamed at Claire.

"Really?"

Claire recalled a brief exchange she'd had with Shelby at Bettina's party and something clicked in her heart. A missing fragment of her identity slipped into place and made her feel whole for the first time in what felt like forever. She belonged here in Charleston in a way that had nothing to do with Linc.

"Yes, really," Sawyer exclaimed. "Isn't that exciting?"

"You have no idea." All at once, Claire burst into tears. For a long moment, she couldn't breathe and her throat hurt too much to get out a word, but she managed to find her voice again. "I can't believe this is real."

"It sure is. Even before you two figured out that you loved each other, I could see that you were special to him. He told me how important this was to you and I'm so glad I was able to help."

"Have you told Linc?" Claire wondered if this was what had caused him to propose. Maybe he'd decided she was suitable after all.

Sawyer shook her head. "I just found out myself not more than half an hour ago. I thought maybe you'd like to be the one to share your news."

"And your mother?"

"Stop worrying about things that don't matter," Sawyer counseled, clearly recognizing what Claire feared. "Linc loves you and that's all there is to it. Neither he nor my mother care where you came from."

Since when?

Claire repressed the thought. If she had any chance of making things work with Linc, she simply had to stop using the gap in their social stations as an excuse to guard herself from getting hurt.

"I know," she said, expelling her breath in a long sigh. "It's just that it's been so long since anyone has made me feel safe and I'm a little skittish."

"Linc is the best guy around."

"You should listen to her," Linc said from the wide arch that led to the hall. He'd followed Honey, who now raced into the room in Claire's direction. "Are you ready to go tell my mother that I've chosen my future bride?" he asked as she scooped her daughter onto her lap and hugged her.

"Are you sure that's what you want?"

"Do you really need to ask?"

Claire glanced down at her jeans and cotton sweater. "I should change my clothes."

"You are beautiful no matter what you're wearing." He took her hand and grazed his lips across her palm, making Claire shiver. "I'll give you ten minutes to change."

While Sawyer entertained Honey, Claire rummaged through her suitcase. She'd bought a beautiful floral dress a week earlier. It wasn't an expensive designer original, but the soft pastel tones brought out the gold highlights in her hair and the wrap style flattered her slim figure.

Claire slipped into the first-floor bathroom and, within the allotted ten minutes, transformed herself from a fearful runaway to a woman ready to face the upcoming challenges and grab the brass ring.

"You look beautiful," Linc said as she reentered the kitchen.

Sawyer had left moments earlier, leaving Claire and

Honey alone with Linc once again. Claire smoothed her palms down the skirt as he approached, keenly aware as he scrutinized every inch of her appearance.

"Do you think your mother will approve?" In truth, she already knew the answer, but her confidence grew beneath Linc's possessive regard.

"Yes."

"Then I guess we'd better go."

"One thing before we do," he said, reaching into his coat pocket. "I have something for you." He displayed a ring box and popped the top. Framed in black velvet was a huge oval-cut diamond set on a thin rose gold band of micropave-set diamonds. "Claire Robbins, will you marry me?"

This time she didn't have to think about the answer. "Linc Thurston, I love you with all my heart and want to be your wife."

She took his face in her hands as he leaned down to kiss her. Distantly, she heard Honey's sweet giggle. Then she was swept into the heat and wonder of the connection she always felt with him and all her fears melted away.

Both of them were breathing a little unsteadily when they broke off the kiss. Honey was growing impatient, her calls penetrating the fog of passion that had enveloped them. Claire watched while Linc slid the diamond ring onto her left hand, her heart stopping at the joy glinting in his eyes.

How had she gotten so lucky to win this man's heart?

On the way to his mother's house, Claire sat paralyzed, fearing that if she moved a single muscle, the whole thing would vanish like a beautiful dream.

Yet with each block they traversed, alarm zinged with ever-increasing speed along Claire's nerves until by the time they pulled into his mother's driveway she was buzzing with tension.

"Relax," Linc murmured as he turned off the car. "No one is going to eat you alive."

"That's easy for you to say," she retorted more sharply than she intended. "You're wealthy and socially prominent. I'm a nobody who cleans your house."

His eyebrows rose at her vehemence, but then he nodded. "Thanks for reminding me. There's something I forgot to do." He flashed her a mischievous grin. "You're fired."

Taking his dismissal in the manner he intended, she smiled in return. "I've never been fired from a job before."

"Never?"

"I'm an exceptional employee. Every boss I've ever worked for has given me glowing performance reviews."

"Of course they have," he murmured in a fond tone.

Linc opened his car door and started to get out but then noticed that she hadn't moved. He reached out and caught her hand, giving her fingers a gentle squeeze. "Come on."

She slipped from the car and went to stand on the brick walkway that stretched from the driveway to the front door while Linc got Honey from her car seat. He moved with confidence and care, having done this dozens of times.

Claire then realized how long this moment had been coming. She just hadn't seen it. Linc had never been just her employer. He'd been her friend. Someone who cared about her and Honey, who'd invited himself into her life.

This flash of insight bolstered her courage. She would face his mother with her head high, confident in the knowledge that she was the woman he loved and intended to marry.

"It's about time you arrived," Bettina called from the living room. "Sawyer tells me you two are engaged."

Claire glanced at Linc as the three of them crossed the threshold and entered the room. The next ten minutes would tell her how the rest of her life would play out. Linc gave her a reassuring smile before answering his mother.

"We are, indeed," Linc said, his satisfaction bolstering Claire.

If this amazing man loved her, she could face whatever the future held.

"Wonderful." Bettina got to her feet as they neared and her gaze met Claire's. She held out her arms and Claire hesitated only a second before stepping into the older woman's embrace. "I just know you and Linc will be so very happy together," she whispered, giving Claire a hard hug before letting her go.

"Thank you," Claire murmured, overwhelmed by a flood of emotions.

Bettina sat down as Dolly appeared with a bottle of champagne and crystal flutes.

"We are going to plan the most lavish wedding this town has seen in years," Linc's mother stated. "Claire will have a dozen bridesmaids and the most expensive gown we can find."

While Bettina began mulling over ideas for the venue and potential wedding planners, Claire sipped her champagne and held Linc's hand. A surge of fondness and belonging flooded her as she realized the acceptance and family she'd craved for so long were going to be hers.

"Thank you," she murmured, resting her head on his arm.

"For what?"

"Making me a part of your family. I love you so much." She tilted her head back and met his gaze. "I never thought I could be as happy as I am right now."

"I'm the lucky one. We belong together. You and Honey make my life complete." He leaned down and placed a soft kiss on her lips.

"I like belonging with you," she agreed, thinking how the Robbins family had come full circle now that she'd returned to Charleston.

She couldn't wait until she and Linc were alone so she could share with him what Sawyer had found out. Yet as excited as she was by the news that she had a connection to the Charleston elite, it no longer determined who she was. For that, all she needed to do was gaze into Linc's blue eyes to see her true self reflected there. His love was all she needed to accept that she was exactly where she should be.

* * * * *

#2587 AN HONORABLE SEDUCTION
The Westmoreland Legacy • by Brenda Jackson
Navy SEAL David "Flipper" Holloway has one mission: get close to gorgeous store owner Swan Jamison and find out all he can. But flirtation leads to seduction and he's about to get caught between duty and the woman he vows to claim as his...

#2588 REUNITED...WITH BABY
Texas Cattleman's Club: The Impostor • by Sara Orwig
Wealthy tech tycoon Luke has come home and he'll do whatever it takes to revive his family's ranch. Even hire the woman he left behind, veterinarian and single mother Scarlett. He can't say yes to forever, but will one more night be enough?

#2589 THE TWIN BIRTHRIGHT
Alaskan Oil Barons • by Catherine Mann
When reclusive inventor Royce Miller is reunited with his ex-fiancée and her twin babies in a snowstorm, he vows to protect them at all costs—even if the explosive chemistry that drove them apart is stronger than ever!

#2590 THE ILLEGITIMATE BILLIONAIRE
Billionaires and Babies • by Barbara Dunlop
Black sheep Deacon Holt, illegitimate son of a billionaire, must marry the gold-digging widow of his half brother if he wants his family's recognition. Actually desiring the beautiful single mother isn't part of the plan, especially when she has shocking relevations of her own...

#2591 WRONG BROTHER, RIGHT MAN
Switching Places • by Kat Cantrell
To inherit his fortune, flirtatious Valentino LeBlanc must swap roles with his too-serious brother. He'll prove he's just as good as, if not better than, his brother. At everything. But when he hires his brother's ex to advise him, things won't stay professional for long...

#2592 ONE NIGHT TO FOREVER
The Ballantyne Billionaires • by Joss Wood
When Lachlyn is outed as a long-lost Ballantyne heiress, wealthy security expert Reame vows to protect her. She's his best friend's sister, an innocent... Surely he can keep his hands to himself. But all it takes is one night to ignite a passion that could burn them both...

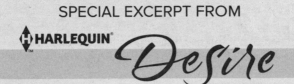
That damn buzz passed from him to her and ignited the
flames low in her belly.

"When I get back to the office, you will officially
become a client," Reame said in a husky voice. "But
you're not my client…yet."

His words made no sense, but she did notice that he
was looking at her like he wanted to kiss her.

Reame gripped her hips. She felt his heat and…
Wow…

God and heaven.

Teeth scraped and lips soothed, tongues swirled and
whirled, and heat, lazy heat, spread through her limbs
and slid into her veins. Reame was kissing her, and time
and space shifted.

It felt natural for her legs to wind around his waist, to
lock her arms around his neck and take what she'd been
fantasizing about. Kissing Reame was better than she'd
imagined—she was finally experiencing all those fuzzy
feels romance books described.

It felt perfect. It felt right.

Reame jerked his mouth off hers and their eyes connected, his intense, blazing with hot green fire.

She wanted him… She never wanted anybody. And never this much.

"Holy crap—"

Reame stiffened in her arms and Lachlyn looked over his shoulder to the now-open door to where her brother stood, half in and half out of the room. Lachlyn slid down Reame's hard body. She pushed her bangs off her forehead and released a deep breath, grateful that Reame shielded her from Linc.

Lachlyn touched her swollen lips and glanced down at her chest, where her hard nipples pushed against the fabric of her lacy bra and thin T-shirt. She couldn't possibly look more turned-on if she tried.

Lachlyn couldn't look at her brother, but he sounded thoroughly amused. "Want me to go away and come back in fifteen?"

Reame looked at her and, along with desire, she thought she saw regret in his eyes. He slowly shook his head. "No, we're done."

Lachlyn met his eyes and nodded her agreement.

Yes, they were done. They had to be.

Don't miss
ONE NIGHT TO FOREVER by Joss Wood,
part of her **BALLANTYNE BILLIONAIRES** *series!*

Available May 2018 wherever
Harlequin® Desire books and ebooks are sold.

www.Harlequin.com

HDEXP0418

Want to give in to temptation with
steamy tales of irresistible desire?

Check out **Harlequin® Presents®**,
Harlequin® Desire and
Harlequin® Kimani™ Romance books!

New books available every month!

CONNECT WITH US AT:

Harlequin.com/Community

 Facebook.com/HarlequinBooks

Twitter.com/HarlequinBooks

Instagram.com/HarlequinBooks

Pinterest.com/HarlequinBooks

ReaderService.com

**ROMANCE WHEN
YOU NEED IT**

PGENRE2017

LOVE
Harlequin
romance?

Join our Harlequin community to share your thoughts and connect with other romance readers!

Be the first to find out about promotions, news, and exclusive content!

Sign up for the Harlequin e-newsletter and download a free book from any series at

www.TryHarlequin.com

CONNECT WITH US AT:

Harlequin.com/Community

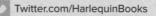 Facebook.com/HarlequinBooks

Twitter.com/HarlequinBooks

Instagram.com/HarlequinBooks

Pinterest.com/HarlequinBooks

ReaderService.com

 **HARLEQUIN**®

**ROMANCE WHEN
YOU NEED IT**

HSOCIAL2017